Caught Inside

By

Lynnette Beers

ISBN 978-1-949096-37-8

Cover Design by AcornGraphics

Editors Verda Foster and Zee Ahmad

Publisher's Note:

Acknowledgements

First and foremost, I would like to thank Patty Schramm from Flashpoint Publications for helping me get this book published. To my amazing editors, Verda Foster and Zee Ahmad: I express my gratitude for your expertise and support in the final stages of publication. I am grateful also to Ann McMan for creating such an amazing book cover. Once again, you nailed it.

I am deeply indebted to my beta readers—Nicole Falconer, Robert Falconer, Sallyanne Monti, Christina Short, and Lisa Turnbull. You provided valuable feedback during the revision process. I also want to thank Barbara Clanton and Jennifer Fenwick for advice as I revised the book.

I would also like to recognize the Laguna Beach Marine Safety Department for the helpful information your guards provided about surfing and ocean rescue procedures.

Additionally, I'm grateful for assistance from Diane Gillespie and Vara Neverow from the International Virginia Woolf Society in guiding me in the right direction to get permission to use excerpts from Virginia Woolf's novels.

Also, I am grateful for the assistance from Greg Kahn, Zenna Hurley MacGregor, and Jay Wittkop for their help in coming up with the right Hawaiian phrases used in my book.

Additionally, I express my gratitude to the locals on the island of Molokai who assisted me as I edited this novel.

In addition, I wish to say a special *mahalo nui loa* to my father, Robert Beers, for teaching me about Hawaiian customs and traditions that he learned as a boy growing up in Hawaii.

Furthermore, I am especially grateful for the help from Karen Sandore, one of the best nurses in the medical field. Thank you for the helpful information about meds and medical procedures.

To my brother, cousins, and my closest friends: I'm thankful for your support and encouragement over the years. You always remind me to never stop dreaming.

And finally, to Kat: Thank you for your continual love and support as I write my novels. You have believed in me as a writer from the start, and for that I am truly grateful.

Dedication

This book is dedicated to all LGBTQ+ teenagers who have ever felt lost or alone. Find your allies… We've got your back.

"Friendship is a sheltering tree."—Samuel Taylor Coleridge

Chapter One

Clear Springs Lake, Mississippi: July 1996

Maddie could barely see the ground. The sun had set well over an hour ago. The damp board shorts and tank top provided no protection from the cool night breeze. Twigs scraped her arms and legs as she carefully scurried through the woods. A blanket of stars and the crescent moon provided just enough light for her to see Brooke Robbins, a camp counselor, a couple paces ahead. If they could only figure out how to get to Clear Springs Lake, they'd be able to find their way back to camp.

The bell from the camp lodge rang out in the distance. It started clanging not long after sunset. Every few minutes, the bell gonged for several minutes straight. Then silence for a couple minutes. Then the gonging would continue.

Normally used to call the campers to the dining hall, tonight the clangs sounded ominous—and far away. Each strike of the bell only escalated Maddie's disorientation and fear. She swallowed, but the lump in her throat refused to go away. Though she'd been coming to Camp Wallace for the past six years, this was the first time she'd been away from the cabins at night. Nothing looked like she remembered it.

Maddie stopped walking and peered into the dark woods. "Do you think we should head up this hill? Maybe that leads to the main road. Or maybe we should turn back around. There could be another campground nearby."

Brooke stepped closer, her hand brushing Maddie's arm. "I think we should keep going this way. This feels like the right way. I've been in these woods several times. Just…not at night." Brooke pulled her hand away and trudged on ahead.

Maddie wasn't sure she agreed. Maybe they should instead remain where they were and hope the rescuers found them. But something rustled in the underbrush, and Maddie scampered after her friend. She did her best to put all her faith in Brooke to find their way through the forest and return to camp.

They weren't supposed to leave the campsite after dinner, but

Brooke had invited Maddie to go for a walk along the lake. Maddie really liked Brooke. Whenever they spent time together, they'd talk and laugh nonstop, leaving Maddie so happy. Maddie had suggested they go for a dip in the lake, since the early evening had been warm. After their swim, Brooke suggested they pick wild berries in the woodsy area beyond the lake. They'd strolled several yards from the main campsite and lost their sense of direction once it got dark. How foolish they were to have wandered from camp without flashlights.

With no clear trail, they pushed through shrubs and low-hanging branches. Neither spoke as they searched for Clear Springs Lake, where they'd be able to follow the water's edge back to camp. Damp strands of hair chilled Maddie's bare shoulders. Her cheap flip-flops crunched over pinecones and twigs, but she solidly trudged ahead until she smacked her shin on a fallen log. Maddie yelped loudly, and Brooke rushed to her side.

"What happened? You okay?" Brooke's voice was calm and steady, sounding more like an adult than a teenaged counselor.

"I walked right into a log." Maddie winced in pain as blood trickled down her leg. The gash in her shin must be deep. "Seems like the bell is getting faint. Maybe we should go back up the hill."

Brooke set her hand on the small of Maddie's back and guided her to a boulder where they sat down. "We have to keep heading toward the lake. It's where they're probably searching for us. But let's take a short break to rest."

Exhausted and cold, Maddie leaned closer to Brooke, who wrapped an arm around her. It was too dark to see Brooke clearly, but her warm breath gently brushing her neck calmed Maddie a bit.

"We're gonna be okay," Brooke said quietly, and gently rubbed Maddie's back.

Maddie had gone to Camp Wallace since she was eight, but now at age fourteen, she related more to sixteen-year-old Brooke than she did the other campers. Once they discovered they both lived in Ellisville and would be going to the same high school in the fall, they'd become close.

They rested for a few minutes and resumed trudging through the woods. As they wove through the thick vegetation, Maddie counted each faint clang of the bell. One, two, three... By the time she got to twenty, she lost count. The sound seemed farther away now. Did the gongs come from behind them? From over the ridge? From across the lake?

"How long will they keep ringing the bell?" Maddie's voice quivered as she blinked back the tears.

"Until we're found." Brooke said this so matter-of-factly, like she wasn't a bit scared about being lost.

Maddie lost her footing on some loose gravel and grabbed Brooke's arm for support. "What if they don't find us?"

"They'll find us. I mean, at least by morning when the sun's up. Last year when I went through orientation, they told us about the different bell signals used at camp. You know, when it's time to wake up or when it's time for dinner. Right now, it's obviously a distress signal, but they're not gonna give up."

"But we…we're gonna freeze if we're stuck out here all night." Maddie's teeth chattered, and she couldn't stop shaking. Though she wanted to believe Brooke, she feared the worst—that they'd be stranded out here all night long and get frostbite.

"It only goes down to around sixty at night in the summer. We'll be fine. Besides, they're bound to find us soon."

"How do you know that?"

Brooke turned to face Maddie and took hold of her hands, giving them a quick squeeze. "Since when has Maddie Fong been a wuss?" Her tone was playful. "Didn't you swim to the other side of the lake with me yesterday? And only a little while ago you went for a swim at dusk."

Maddie loved how Brooke said her full name, as if she was someone special and not just one of the campers. "That was different. It was still light out when we swam. It's totally dark right now, and we can't even see where we're going."

"Ever since I met you last year, I always saw you as fearless. The key to survival is not to panic." Brooke squeezed Maddie's hands once more before releasing them and continuing down the hill. "We can't be that far from camp. Once we make our way through these trees, we'll find our way back to the lake."

Maddie gripped tree trunks and branches as she scaled down the hill after Brooke. With each step, the pain from the gash in her shin radiated up to her thigh.

"Wait!" Brooke stopped walking. "Did you hear that?"

Maddie strained to hear something other than the distant peal of the bell or the occasional hoot from an owl or the wind through the trees. Then, she heard it—the faint sound of people's voices calling their names in the distance.

"They're coming for us," Brooke said then picked up her pace. "A search and rescue team is probably at the bottom of the ridge. See, I told you they'd find us. Hey, over here! We're heading toward you!"

"Help! Don't go away!" Maddie hollered.

Brooke continued to yell as she barreled down the steep ravine. Even though Maddie's legs were raw from the twigs and branches, and the gash in her shin stung, she did her best to keep up.

"Over here!" Maddie yelled, her throat raspy and sore.

The terrain got steeper and rockier, and Maddie slowed her pace. By now, Brooke was far ahead, but she was at least within shouting range.

"Hey, we're up here! Maddie, I think I see the lights from camp on the other side of the lake."

"We need help! Up here!" Hoarse from screaming to alert the rescuers, Maddie hoped they'd be found soon.

Unsure how they'd managed to wander all the way to the other side of Clear Springs Lake, Maddie took careful steps down the ravine. A grouping of large rocks blocked the path, and she relied on touch alone to climb over them. The entire area was uneven and gravelly. One false step, and she'd tumble down the hill.

Maddie didn't have Brooke's uncanny ability to easily make her way through the dark. Though she no longer heard the rescuers calling their names, Maddie continued to make her way down to the lake. She wanted nothing more than a sip of water and a warm bed. Maddie wove through the pine trees with her hands outstretched to make sure no other rocks were in the way. But then, Brooke yelled from a few yards away. Then she screamed. And screamed again.

Maddie froze in her tracks and gripped tightly to a branch. "Brooke, what happened?"

"Ah, shit! I hurt my leg."

"Keep talking. I'm coming to you." Maddie listened for the location of Brooke's voice, carefully making her way through the trees and rocks until she found Brooke on the ground, hunched over.

Brooke rocked back and forth as she held her right leg. "I tumbled down the hill. Then I whacked my leg on a big rock. It was wedged between a couple rocks, but I managed to pull it out. I might've broken my leg."

"Broke it?" Maddie crouched at Brooke's side to try and see how bad the injury was.

"Well, more like mangled it in between two rocks when I fell. It's bleeding pretty bad."

"I should go on ahead and find my way to the rescuers, and they can come get you."

"No, we shouldn't separate. I'll be fine. I just need you to give me a hand so I can stand up and get to the lake. It's only a few yards away. The search and rescue team will have a better chance of finding us if we stay by the lake."

Maddie squinted between the trees. There did appear to be a black body of water ahead. But no signs of the rescuers. She didn't see anyone with flashlights and no longer heard their voices. The sound of the bell was so faint that she wondered if she'd imagined hearing it. But there were dim lights way on the other side of the lake. If not Camp Wallace, it was probably another campsite or a house.

Maddie stood behind Brooke, gripped her hands under her armpits, and used all her strength to help her stand. When Brooke cried out from the pain, Maddie secured both arms around her body and helped her take slow steps down the hill. Within a few minutes, they finally reached level ground and stood a few feet from the lake. Now that they were at the water's edge, Maddie was a bit more hopeful they'd be found. She eased Brooke onto the ground and crouched down to get a better look at her leg. She didn't need to see clearly to know Brooke needed medical attention. So much blood oozed from the wound.

"You're gonna be okay." Maddie set a hand on Brooke's knee and hollered out again with hopes of the rescuers hearing her faint voice. "Help! We're over here!"

Brooke slipped her hand in Maddie's, her skin cold but her grasp firm. "I'm sorry I got us lost. All I wanted to do was spend time alone with you away from the others. The camp director is pretty strict about us not forming close friendships with any of the campers, but we always have fun together. You're the only other person who's willing to go for a swim at dusk."

Though surprised Brooke held her hand, Maddie loved how it felt—her skin so soft and amazing. The firm grip made her feel safe. "Next summer, I'll be old enough to be one of the camp counselors. I won't just be one of the kids at camp."

"Next year when you're one of the counselors, we can ask to be in the same cabin."

"That'd be cool." Maddie let out a nervous laugh. A strange fluttery feeling washed over her and settled in her stomach. Ever since last year, she was drawn to Brooke's warmth and kindness and wanted to be around her all the time, but they shouldn't have wandered off alone. Maddie wanted nothing more than to keep hold of Brooke's hand and never let go. But what she wanted wasn't important right now. Her priority was getting Brooke medical aid.

Brooke squeezed Maddie's hand. "I don't care what the camp director says. Once we get back to camp, we can hang out all we want. I really, really like hanging out with you. I just hope they find us soon."

Maddie set her other hand on Brooke's arm. "I like hanging out with you, too. They'll find us. They're probably closer than we think. Once you're home and recuperating from this stupid injury, maybe I can come to your house and keep you company."

"That'd be fun." Brooke laughed softly and released Maddie's hand.

Maddie stood up. "Stay here and rest your leg. I'm going to walk along the shore, see if I can find someone."

"Don't leave me alone—wait, I think I see some people in the distance." Brooke winced in pain when she tried to stand. "Hey, over here!"

Maddie caught a glimpse of what looked like beams from flashlights, but she was sure the search and rescue people were too far away for them to hear her. "I'm going to go back along the shore to try and get their attention."

"No, stay with me. Help me into the water." Brooke made another attempt to stand but quickly sat back down and cried out in pain.

"Into the *water*? You said we should wait here until they find us."

"You can see they've already left this area and will soon be too far to see us. We have to swim to the other side. It's our only chance."

"If you can barely walk, how are you gonna swim all the way to the other side?"

"I don't need my legs to swim." Brooke began pulling herself along the sand. "I can make it just using my arms. Been on the swim team long enough to know I can do the breaststroke all the way to the other side."

Trying to make it to the other side of the lake was a bad idea. Even swimming a few yards in the cold water late at night would be foolish.

But before Maddie could convince Brooke that they should remain where they were, Brooke crawled to the edge of the lake and entered the water.

"Maddie, come on!" Brooke was now a few feet from the shore. "It's our only chance of them finding us tonight."

This was a really dumb thing to do, but she couldn't leave Brooke out there on her own. Maddie wedged her flip-flops in the waist of her board shorts and waded into the lake. The cold water stung the scrapes on her arms and the gash on her shin, but she dove underneath and swam toward Brooke. Both of them remained quiet as they made their way to the other side of the lake.

There was no sign of their rescuers. Maddie's body tensed from the frigid temperature. The wind started to pick up, the lake quickly becoming choppy. Her strength was fading, but then she heard Brooke cough and gasp for air a couple yards away.

"I can't—I can't stay afloat. I thought I could do it. I thought I could swim to the other side, but now I don't think I can—" Her head started to dip under the waves.

"Brooke!" Maddie slashed her hands and kicked with all her might to reach her. In the distance, she caught a glimpse of flash-lights—but the beams were focused on the woods, not the shore. She returned her attention to Brooke, who was gone.

"Brooke!" Maddie screamed. She dove below and blindly searched for her. When Maddie returned to the surface, she called out Brooke's name a couple more times but still couldn't find her. Once again, Maddie went below the surface and reached out her arms in an attempt to locate Brooke. She saw nothing but pitch-black and emerged only to see the grey surface of the lake. No signs of Brooke anywhere. The silence was eerie and lonely. Maddie shivered as she continued her search.

Finally, the sounds of splashing alerted Maddie to Brooke flailing wildly a few feet away. Maddie swam over and grabbed her arm, doing her best to keep Brooke afloat, but she was exhausted and cold. Barely able to keep both their chins above water, Maddie tried to figure out the closest way to get to shore. But Brooke continued to flounder, and she pulled Maddie under.

Never was Maddie more terrified than in this moment. She was normally a decent swimmer, but never had to struggle against another person's weight just to stay afloat. She was running out of air and getting weaker. Finding her way to the surface was crucial, or they'd both drown. From somewhere, she summoned the strength to kick, and the two of them emerged, gasping for air. When Maddie tried to take another deep breath, she inhaled water and coughed. Her lungs burned as she attempted to catch her breath. Brooke thrashed but more weakly this time, and Maddie tried to tread water to keep them both afloat.

The muscles in Maddie's legs spasmed. Brooke trembled in Maddie's arms. Maybe she'd gone into shock? Or she'd lost so much blood that she'd soon lose consciousness? Was this the moment they both drowned?

With Brooke no longer flailing, Maddie was able to turn on her back and float. She looped an arm under Brooke's armpit and pulled her across her chest. With a feeble kick of her weary legs, she got them moving and prayed she could get them to shore soon. Brooke didn't say a word, and Maddie couldn't spare the breath to ask if she was still conscious. With her free arm, Maddie slapped another weak backstroke at the surface of the water and then another, hoping the motion would pull them toward shore.

When Maddie first heard the voices, she wasn't sure if it was her imagination or not.

"Brooke!" That sounded like a man.

"Maddie!" That was a woman. "You out there? We're from search and rescue."

Maddie turned her head to see several flashlights aimed at her and Brooke. She didn't let go of Brooke, but she knew she couldn't make it to shore without help.

"Please, somebody!" Maddie managed to say, her voice feeble.

Someone on the shore yelled something, but it was garbled by a wave sloshing against Maddie's ear. Somebody from the search and rescue team was swimming out to them with smooth, rapid strokes. A couple people followed close behind.

"We've got you, you're safe now," a man said.

Someone took Brooke from her, and another person gripped Maddie's arm and buoyed her up. She almost sobbed in relief as her rescuer—the woman who'd yelled her name—quickly swam her to shore and helped her walk out of the lake. A couple of guys set Maddie atop some sort of rigid board.

"I take it one of you is Maddie Fong, and the other is Brooke Robbins?" A man shone a flashlight on Maddie's face. "We been looking for the two of you for over three hours. You're safe now. You injured?"

"Just a gash on my leg." Maddie squinted from the bright light and tried to look next to her to see how Brooke was doing. "Brooke hurt her leg. She thinks it's broken. She bled a lot, and then she got really weak as we tried to swim across the lake. I knew we shouldn't have gone in the lake. We should've—"

"Hon, we're gonna get you both to a hospital soon." The woman wrapped a crinkly blanket over Maddie. "Y'all are safe now. They're working on Brooke right now."

Maddie couldn't stop shivering. "I'm really not that hurt. Probably just need to clean the gash and cover it with a bandage."

"Stay with us, Brooke," a man said.

Maddie gasped and reached out for Brooke, but the woman gently held her back.

"I'm Tammy, an EMT. These guys are from search and rescue." Tammy crouched down next to Maddie, pulled the blanket away from her leg, and wrapped something around the wound. "We'll get you to the main road soon. Once there, we'll contact your parents just as soon as we get to an area where we can get cell service. I'm sure they'll wanna drive out here tonight to bring you back home."

Maddie started to cry. Her mom would be so freaked out. As an only child in a single parent household, she often faced strict rules from her overprotective mother. "It's just my mom. We live a couple hours from Camp Wallace. I think I'll be fine to stay at camp tonight, but what about Brooke? Is she gonna be okay?"

Tammy placed a thick blanket over Maddie's torso. "We're

doing everything we can to stabilize her. She's in good hands now. She might've gone into shock from the loss of blood or maybe started to experience the first signs of hypothermia from being in the cold lake for too long. Hang in there, kiddo. You're gonna be okay."

"We need to get her to a hospital fast," a man said. "I can barely get a pulse."

"We'll follow the lake until we get to the nearest campsite." Tammy secured a strap around Maddie's body. "There's a utility road up ahead."

The rescuers lifted the body board, and all Maddie could see was the starlit sky. As they lugged her body over the uneven terrain, Maddie finally warmed up and started to get sleepy. The clanging bell slowly got louder the longer they walked.

The rescuers clomped over a narrow bridge next to the lake. Maddie couldn't believe she and Brooke were this close to the bridge the entire time they were lost. She craned her neck to catch a glimpse of what was happening. Several emergency vehicles waited up ahead in a dirt parking lot. The flashing red lights from a fire truck lit up the surface of the lake—the water ominous and dangerous.

The rescuers transferred Brooke to a gurney and moved her closer to an ambulance. Glaring light from the back of the opened door to the ambulance shone brightly where Maddie lay atop the backboard. Brooke lay limp on the gurney as a paramedic wrapped a blood pressure cuff around her arm. Tammy loosened the strap around Maddie's body and helped her sit up.

"I've stabilized the bleeding," a paramedic said. "But she's showing signs of hypothermia."

Another guy tucked a blanket around Brooke's body. "Her blood pressure is dropping."

"Ah, shit," Tammy said under her breath. She took a few steps closer to the ambulance and set her hands on her hips. "Probably from being in that damn lake for so long. I'm surprised both of them don't have hypothermia."

The voices of the paramedics blended together, their tone urgent yet controlled. Maddie couldn't stop her body from shaking.

"Her BP is continuing to drop," one of them said.

One of the paramedics inserted an IV into Brooke's arm.

"Better notify the camp to help us get in touch with her parents. We need to transport her now."

The paramedics hoisted the gurney into the ambulance and climbed inside. One of them shut the door, the sound echoing across the dirt parking lot and to the lake.

Maddie attempted to stand, but she became lightheaded and slumped on the ground. "Wait, I have to go with her!" Though she couldn't stop her body from shivering, she again attempted to stand.

Tammy gripped Maddie's arm and sat her down on the hard dirt. "Hon, you need to stay here."

"Can't you let me ride in the ambulance with her?" Maddie started to cry again, her body shaking with each sob.

Tammy crouched on the ground and draped an arm around Maddie's shoulders. "They're doing the best they can to help Brooke. Let's tend to your wounds."

The ambulance pulled away, the flashing red and white lights strobing over the lake. Sirens wailed in the distance, the sound getting fainter by the second. Maddie leaned forward and hugged her knees as she rocked back and forth. The crescent moon cast a faint light over Clear Springs Lake. Maddie knew she'd never enter that water ever again—not tomorrow or next week or even next summer.

Chapter Two

San Clemente, California: August 1996

Maddie had been right. She never would enter Clear Springs Lake again, because her mother had decided the two of them needed to move to California. Though she didn't miss that lake, Maddie did miss her friends back home. Especially Brooke.

With the car barely moving, the air was hot and stagnant. Maddie stuck her face out the passenger window and inhaled the humid marine air. Though still overheated, she slumped back in her seat as she hung her right arm out the window. "It's so hot here. Can we stop the car and get some ice cream?"

Her mother shook her head. "I told you, we're almost there, and I don't control the weather. We've been on the road for days, and you barely said a word. Now all you've done for the past two hours is complain."

"We've hardly stopped except to get gas and stay in boring motels and eat bad food from greasy diners."

"Honey, the sooner we get there, the sooner we'll be able to get settled in our new town. Won't it be fun to enjoy a nice dinner tonight after we unload the car?"

"Yeah, whatever." Maddie spread a huge map on her lap and checked off the states they'd passed through: Louisiana, Texas, New Mexico, Arizona, and now, California. On the map, Mississippi seemed so far from where they were right now. Maddie blinked away tears as she thought about how she was five whole states away from home.

Her mom ended up on the wrong freeway this afternoon but eventually found her way to the coast. They motored through cities Maddie had never heard of: Newport Beach, Corona Del Mar, Laguna Beach, Dana Point. Now in San Clemente, they followed the long stretch of Pacific Coast Highway until the road narrowed.

On Maddie's right, the wide expanse of the Pacific Ocean stretched out as far as her eyes could see. A few yards off shore, surfers and boogie boarders rode the waves next to the pier. She'd never seen an ocean this clear—the white breakers a striking contrast to the teal waters. Way past the pier, bigger waves headed toward shore. Surely only brave swimmers and surfers went out that far. Memories of that awful night in Clear Springs Lake came flooding back, and she shuddered.

So many people frolicked in the ocean and on the beach that it made this place look frenzied—far different than what Maddie experienced back home in the South. The bright sand blinded her as the car crept down the coast in bumper-to-bumper traffic. Maddie heard the squeals of kids playing in the surf and the thud of music from boomboxes. A few guys tossed a football back and forth while women in skimpy bathing suits sat nearby to watch. Maddie never saw girls in tiny bikinis in Mississippi, where the closest ocean was nearly two hours away. On the rare occasion when her mother drove them to the Gulf on a humid summer day, Maddie seldom put her feet in the water since the ocean always looked so murky—a stark contrast to the inviting blue of California waters.

Maddie dropped the map to the floorboard, unclasped her seatbelt, and leaned against the passenger door. She rested her elbows on the opened window and let her long hair catch in the wind.

Her mom tugged on Maddie's T-shirt. "Maddie, put your seatbelt back on right now. California law says all passengers must wear seatbelts while the car is in motion. I don't want to get a ticket the first day we're here."

The fresh air cooled and soothed Maddie's skin, but she had no plans to move away from the window. "We're not even moving. We've only gone a few feet in the last half hour."

"Madelyn Joan Fong, you're gettin' on my last nerve. Put your seatbelt on and get your head away from the window. Your hair's a mess."

"Okay, Angela May Fong." Maddie hung her arm out the window.

"Maddie, don't you sass me. Roll up that window right now. You have to look nice when we see Popo. You need to look presentable when we get to her house. It's our house now, too."

While she gazed at the shimmering ocean, Maddie hesitantly put the seatbelt back on and rolled up the window. When Mom used her full name, it meant she was really upset. With the windows up, the car quickly heated up. The AC had stopped working all the way back in Texas.

"I still don't understand why we have to live with Popo and Auntie." Maddie watched surfers ride the waves to shore. After five o'clock now, the sand was still covered by beach towels, chairs, and barbeques. If the beach was this crowded in the evening, then Maddie didn't want to have anything to do with it even in the day.

"Popo's getting older. She's lonely now."

"But Auntie and her kids are with her. Uncle Jeff, too. How can Popo be lonely with so many people in her house? She's got three grandkids at home with her. Why would she want another one there?"

"Family is everything to Popo, but Auntie and Uncle Jeff are busy. Popo needs my help running the restaurant. You'll work there, too."

"You're not gonna teach anymore?"

"Well, not right now. I reckon I'll help Popo run the restaurant during the next school year, and then maybe I'll see if I can get a job at one of the local elementary schools once I get a teaching credential in California. Or maybe I won't ever go back to teaching. It'll depend on if we can help Popo get Royal Palace thriving again. Maybe Popo and I can come up with some new dishes to add to the menu."

Maddie didn't mind her grandmother's cooking once in a while, and it was always fun to go to Royal Palace when they were in town, but to eat Chinese food all the time would be boring. She hoped she could still eat fried chicken and grits like they did back home. Her mom had broken the news of them moving to California only two weeks ago. With barely enough time to say goodbye to her friends, Maddie wondered if Brooke would keep in touch like she said she'd do.

She reached into her backpack and pulled out the letter she'd finished writing last night. As she ran her finger over Brooke's name on the front of the envelope, Maddie fought back the tears. Why did they have to move? She wouldn't know anyone at her new school. Maybe Mom would regret moving to Southern California, and they'd be back next year. Maddie would then be able to go to the same high school as Brooke. Though she and Brooke promised to write each other often, Maddie vowed to save money to make long-distance phone calls with hopes of bridging the distance between California and Mississippi.

When her grandfather died last year, Maddie and her mother visited Popo three times in just one year. But Maddie never expected they'd move to San Clemente to live with her grandmother. Popo would carry on long conversations with her in broken English mixed with Chinese. Although only able to speak certain phrases in Chinese, Maddie understood some of what Popo said but usually answered her in English. One day, Maddie hoped to meet her other grandparents. All she knew was that they were white Southern folks like her dad, nothing like Popo. Her mother was tight-lipped about them, and any time Maddie pressed her for more information, she said she had no idea where they lived.

"When the restaurant does better, can we move into our own house?" Maddie asked.

"We'll see, but I think you'll like living with Popo and your cousins." Angela lowered the window on her side. "Lord, it's hotter than Hades here. Maybe your cousins will take you to the beach tomorrow after we unpack. I bet a swim in the ocean will be refreshing. I might even go for a dip before I help Popo at the restaurant."

The current was choppy—way more dangerous than Clear Springs Lake. "I'd rather stay home. The waves look kinda rough here."

"There are plenty of lifeguards here. I'm sure they wouldn't let people swim if it was too dangerous. Looks like a safe beach."

"That's what they said about the lake."

"Honey, it's totally different to swim in the ocean in the daytime than it is to make your way across a lake in the middle of the night when injured and disoriented."

Over the past few weeks, Maddie had often woken up in the middle of the night feeling as if she were drowning. She'd thrash about in the sheets as though she were in the lake with no idea how she'd make it safely to shore. "I wasn't disoriented. I should've stopped Brooke from going into the lake when it was dark out. We should've waited on shore until they found us."

"Well, yes, but you had no clue that her leg was shattered from the fall. You did a brave thing by attempting to swim across the lake with her. It was late at night, and you two were exhausted after finding your way through the forest."

While Maddie's scrapes and bruises were now healed, Brooke had only recently been released from the hospital. After three surgeries and a couple rounds of IV antibiotics, the infection had finally cleared up. Maddie had visited Brooke in the hospital only once, but she wanted to visit her more often and sit with her all day long, maybe hold her hand and comfort her. Perhaps once they got to Popo's house, Maddie could call Brooke and see how she was doing.

Angela reached over to smooth Maddie's hair. "Sweetie, California's a great place to live, especially this area. Popo's house is way up on top of a hill. Remember how you can see clear to the ocean from the backyard?"

"We had a nice place back home, and Aunt Nancy and Uncle Tim lived near us. I don't see why we have to share a house with a bunch of people now."

Aunt Nancy and Uncle Tim were around the same age as her maternal grandma, and they had a huge house with a backyard next to the woods. She never minded visiting Popo for a week or two, but to live with her all the time wouldn't be much fun. The backyard was nothing but a huge slab of cement with a few giant potted plants.

"I bet you'll love your new school. Since Colin's two years older, he can walk you there each morning and home afterward."

"Are you kidding me? I'm going into ninth grade, not elementary school. What's the big deal? I walked to school by myself back home."

"That's because it was a short walk, and it was a familiar route for you. Things are different here. You'll walk to school with Colin, at least for the first few weeks."

"Mom, that's so lame! I don't need an eleventh grader to escort me to school. All Colin wants to do is talk about basketball or surfing. He's so boring. All my cousins are boring."

"Now, don't go pitchin' a hissy fit. California is your home now. I think you'll like it here. For now, we'll have Colin walk you to school. In my opinion, fourteen years old isn't old enough to be walking to a new school by yourself."

"Apparently it's old enough to be working at Royal Palace. Where's my new school at?"

"Honey, you know you shouldn't end a sentence with a preposition."

"That wasn't a sentence. It was a question." She always got annoyed when Mom corrected her grammar.

"Regardless, don't end a sentence or a question with a preposition. The proper question should have been, 'Where is my new school located?' Or, 'In which city is my new school located?' Anyway, the school is close to Popo's house, probably about a fifteen-minute walk. I think you'll like living in Southern California because there will be more people like us here."

"What do you mean? People with southern accents?" Maddie stared at her mother, whose hands were clenched on the steering wheel. Although Maddie didn't think her voice sounded any different, Angela often reminded her that people in other parts of the country spoke differently. Maddie now regularly practiced speaking like they did on television shows made in Hollywood. She didn't want another reason to stand out from the kids at her new school.

Angela cleared her throat and thrummed her fingers on the steering wheel. "No, honey, Asian people like us. Auntie says there are a few other Chinese people in the neighborhood, and the kids at school are from all over the place. China, Vietnam, India, Mexico."

Would there be anyone like her, though? Maddie had the same color hair and skin as her mother, but her facial features didn't look anything like her mom's or grandmother's. Her eyes were round like her dad's, not almond-shaped like Mom's or Popo's, and her hair was wavy instead of straight.

The only photo of her father had been taken a month before he was killed in Beirut. The edges of the photograph were frayed and bent from how often Maddie held and studied it. The faded image of her dad didn't look much like her except the round eyes. Blond and tall, her father stared at the camera, looking ready to fight the enemy. In his military uniform, he seemed serious and distant, like a stranger.

All she knew, besides what he looked like in the photo, was that his name was Ben Rudolph, but Mom rarely told her anything about him except that he was quiet and kind. Maddie tried to imagine what it would've been like to go by Maddie Rudolph, but that last name sounded strange compared to Fong.

Angela gave Maddie a soft smile while the car idled at the stoplight. "Sweetie, you'll have fun with your cousins. They'll be like big brothers and sisters to you."

"It would've been nicer to have an actual brother or sister."

"A lot of kids your age would be thrilled to have so many cousins around."

"They never hang out with me when I'm here. They don't even like me." Maddie would have to share a room with her cousin Jessica. Three years older, Jessica was more like a stranger and didn't look anything like Maddie. With nothing in common but having the same last name, Maddie wouldn't resemble anyone living in that house.

"Honey, you don't know that. Your cousins will look out for you. You'll also have Auntie and Uncle Jeff there to show you around and help you get adjusted to living in California. They're excited to have us here with them."

"It's gonna suck having to share a room with someone. I liked how things were in Mississippi with just you and me in the house." Maddie furrowed her brow and reached to the floorboard for the map of the United States. She studied it carefully as she ran her finger back along the route they'd taken.

"I think you'll like it here. After school, you can go to the beach with your cousins, even if it's just to sit and read a book. It's only a few blocks from Popo's house and close to her restaurant."

Maddie perused the crowded beach with all the blankets, towels, and chairs strewn across the sand. "There's too many people here."

"There *are* too many people here."

"Well, whatever. This beach is lame. There are too many blankets and chairs on the sand. There's no place to sit."

"Sweetie, I know California is a lot different than Mississippi, but…there were too many bad things in Ellisville, things I didn't want you to ever experience. You'll see that there won't be any people here to do us wrong like in the South. Probably should've moved to California years ago when my parents relocated here, but at least we're finally here now."

When Angela turned down a side street and made her way up a steep hill, Maddie peeked at the fading image of the white sand and shimmering ocean behind her. Soon, they parked in front of a drab, tan house with a low brick wall bordering a courtyard. Maddie pushed the heavy car door open but remained in her seat as she surveyed the members of her family lined up to greet them. The U.S. map was still on her lap, so she neatly folded it and slipped it into the front pocket of her backpack. She'd need that one day to find her way back home.

Chapter Three

San Clemente, California: September 1996

"What are you, anyway?"

The boy flung the question just as Maddie bit into a sweet and tangy bean curd stick, her favorite appetizer from Royal Palace. Not sure if the kid was talking to her or someone else, Maddie ignored him and munched on the sticky appetizer while she went back to reading *Treasure Island*.

"I said, what *are* you?" the boy asked again. "You Mexican? Filipino? Asian?"

Maddie stopped chewing and glanced at the kid talking to her. Brian Fluss sat at a table next to her and Ally Flores in science class and often hogged the desk space atop the lab countertops. A blond, freckly, stocky kid, Brian often got in trouble for talking during class. During these first three weeks of school, he'd never actually spoken to her until now.

"Yeah, you, the one eating that smelly food." Brian stepped closer to Maddie and scarfed down a bunch of tater tots.

"What do you mean?" Maddie asked quietly. With her eyes focused on her book, she continued to eat her lunch. Careful to not get the book dirty, she kept the bean curd stick in her right hand and turned the pages with her left.

"Okay, how about we start with an easier question? What…is…your…name?"

"Maddie."

"Your last name."

"You oughta know by now that it's Fong. Mr. Wilkins calls my name right after yours in science class every morning."

Mr. Wilkins, an old, grey teacher way beyond retirement age, called everyone in class "Miss" or "Mister" instead of using their first names, but occasionally he did use their full names when someone like Brian misbehaved or was reckless with the lab equipment and specimens displayed on the counters. Though Maddie was a freshman, she was placed in the higher science class with the sophomores.

"What kind of name is Fong?" Brian shoved more tater tots into his mouth and wiped his lips on the sleeve of his white T-shirt, leaving a smear of ketchup on the light material.

Close to tears, Maddie didn't answer but took another bite of the bean curd stick. The honey-ginger sauce was sticky, but since she didn't have a wet-wipe, she licked the tips of her fingers. The more Brian pestered her, the more she sweated. She stared at her book as she blinked away tears. The cafeteria's air conditioning had stopped working days ago, but it was much too hot to sit outside. By now back home in Ellisville, fall temperatures were crisp, but here in Southern California, the temperature during September hovered around eighty or ninety every day.

"I said, what kind of name is that?" Brian kicked his foot into her chair.

"It's Chinese." Maddie's voice was shrill and quiet.

"Maddie Ching Chong Fong? You don't look Asian."

"My mom's Chinese."

Maddie peeked in the paper sack to see what else Popo packed for today's lunch. There were two greasy eggrolls wrapped in waxed paper and a Twinkie. If Brian saw what was in the bag, he'd make fun of her for eating this type of food. Maddie folded the top of the bag and set the rest of the bean curd stick on a napkin. While she sat with her hands in her lap, careful to not get any honey-ginger sauce on her shorts, she peeked at a group of kids sitting nearby and noticed Ally Flores over in the corner looking her way. Ally frowned slightly and seemed to be watching to see what Brian might do next. Tempted to move to where Ally and the other kids sat, Maddie instead decided to stay here and ignore Brian while she read her book.

Resolved to finish the book by tonight, Maddie returned to the same chapter she'd been trying to read for the past few minutes. Up until last year, she'd only read stories about little girls and horses. *Treasure Island* opened up a whole new world in Maddie's mind—of dangerous adventures on the sea, desert islands, and buried treasure.

Brian leaned against the table, his heavy body causing the table and plastic chairs to move. "What's that thing you're eating?"

"Bean curd sticks. Made with honey and ginger," Maddie said, the last word sounding more like "jin-jar." Although she'd practiced speaking without a Southern accent, Maddie still said some words with the drawl she worked hard at eliminating.

Without making eye contact with Brian, Maddie lifted her hand to lick the sticky sauce from her thumb and forefinger. All she wanted to do was sit in solitude and read more from Robert Louis Stevenson's adventure book.

"Bean turd? Ching Chong Fong eats turds for lunch!" Brian hollered to the kids sitting at the adjacent tables.

"Bean card," Maddie started to say, letting her accent slip out.

"Bean card? Where y'all from?"

"It's called bean curd. It's a type of—"

"Looks gross and smells like shit. The sauce looks like brown crap. Why don't you eat normal food like the rest of us and not stink up the whole cafeteria?"

Maddie hoped everyone would be called back to class soon and that Brian would leave her alone. She missed Brooke and her other friends in Mississippi. She could speak freely and not have to tone down her Southern drawl. None of the kids back home asked her stupid questions about her food or her name. She just wanted to eat her dessert, the one item in the paper sack which was American.

While she sat there stoic and silent, Maddie opened her book to where she'd left off and proceeded to skim the next few sentences:

I had quite forgot the peril that hung over my head and stood craning over the starboard bulwarks and watching the ripples spreading wide before the bows. I might have fallen without a struggle for my life had not a sudden disquietude seized upon me and made me turn my head.

Brian slapped a hand on the table a few inches from Maddie's book. "Don't Chinese people have black hair and slanty eyes?"

Trembling, Maddie kept her eyes on the page and quietly said, "My dad has blond, curly hair. That's why I have wavy hair and not—"

"Your dad's white? With the name Fong? Don't know too many white people with a chink last name."

"It's my mom's last name." Maddie stared at her lap as sweat trickled down her neck.

"Then what's your dad's last name?"

"Rudolph," Maddie said, fearful he'd make fun of that name, too. What could she say to stop him? "My dad's a Marine. He's in Iraq, fighting in the war." She felt bad lying about her dad being in Iraq, but it worked to stop Brian from asking more about him.

"If you're Chinese, then how come you're not eating with chopsticks, Ching Chong Fong?" Brian snatched Maddie's paper sack, opened it, and pulled out a Twinkie. Maddie automatically reached out a hand to take it back but pulled it back. She didn't want to antagonize him further. Maybe he'd leave her alone if she let him have her food.

After Brian tore off the plastic wrap, he glared at Maddie and squeezed the Twinkie, the white filling oozing from the center and seeping out through his clenched fingers. He wolfed down the Twinkie in just two bites and licked the white filling from between his fingers. Brian reached into the sack and retrieved the greasy eggrolls and tossed them on the table. "What kind of crap is this?"

"They're eggrolls from my popo's restaurant." Maddie stared at the eggrolls wrapped in translucent wrap—the grease seeping from the waxed paper and onto the table. She trembled as sweat trickled down her face, but she didn't take her eyes off the rest of her lunch.

"Your poo-poo's restaurant?"

"Popo… It's Chinese for grandma."

"Tomorrow you sit outside so you don't stink up the whole cafeteria with your gross ching chong food." Brian reached down and took her juice box.

Maddie tried to focus on the next passage from *Treasure Island*, but she was startled by an authoritative voice booming behind her.

"Leave her alone!"

It was her cousin Colin. He grabbed Brian by the shoulders, shoved him against the wall, and twisted his T-shirt up to his chin.

"You don't scare me," Brian said through clenched teeth as he glared up at Colin, who was almost a foot taller.

Colin released Brian's shirt and shoved him into a nearby table. "Don't take what's not yours."

Brian staggered back a step and straightened his shirt collar. "I could easily take you down."

"Take me down? Seriously? You should pick on someone your own size, like a third grader. What kind of guy picks on a girl anyway?"

Brian's face puckered up, and his hands balled into fists. Then his face reddened, obscuring the freckles.

"If you ever bother Maddie again, I'll make you sorry you did." Colin folded his arms and glared at Brian. "Don't ever mess with my cousin again. You understand?"

The bell rang, signaling the end of lunch. Brian dropped his fists and stormed off. Colin sat across from Maddie, then pulled a small bag of Mini Chips Ahoy from his pocket and handed it to her. Still trembling, Maddie opened the bag of cookies and popped one in her mouth. She stood and scooted the chair from the table, checking behind her to make sure Brian had left the cafeteria.

Colin pushed himself up from the chair. "If you're still hungry later, I can buy you another bag of cookies. Or we can stop by Circle K on our way home to get whatever you want. Maybe some Hot Cheetos. Just don't tell Popo or your mom."

Maddie nodded, not sure what she was agreeing to: more Chips Ahoy from the vending machine or Hot Cheetos from Circle K. Or maybe she was acknowledging she'd walk home from school with him, even if it meant waiting a couple hours until he finished basketball practice.

"Thank you," Maddie said, so quiet she wasn't sure Colin heard her, but even she heard the Southern twang in those two words.

"That kid's just a wimp." Colin draped his arm around Maddie's shoulders—the first time he'd shown any sort of kinship in public. "Fluss the Wuss is all talk and no action."

"Thanks," Maddie said, her voice now sounding louder and just like any other kid in Southern California.

Ally walked up to Maddie and smiled. "He's definitely a wimp. And a jerk. Just ignore him. That's what I do. Sit with me during lunch tomorrow, okay?"

"Yeah, sure." Maddie averted her eyes from Ally's and stared at the tile floor.

Ally picked up Maddie's book from the table and handed it to her. "So, you're into literature?"

"Yeah, but the things my English teacher assigns are kinda

lame. I read ahead for English because the books are so easy. I'm reading this one for fun."

"Tomorrow I'll show you a cool poem by a poet named Samuel Taylor Coleridge that I'm reading for my honor's English class. It's kind of like *Treasure Island*. It's about a man who went on an ocean journey."

Intrigued by the mention of this poet, Maddie smiled as she took in Ally's kind face. She'd only spoken to Ally a couple times during science class, but she'd never noticed her pretty green eyes or her sweet smile until now. Maybe lunchtime here wouldn't be so bad after all.

Other kids brushed past Maddie, but Ally remained next to her. With the book tucked under her arm and her backpack slung over her shoulder, Maddie left the cafeteria with Ally and Colin by her side. She shuffled down the hallway with the other students—the kids all strangers. Maybe by the end of the school year she'd blend in with the rest of them. But at least she now had one new friend.

Chapter Four

San Clemente, California: December 1996

While Maddie folded the salmon-colored take-out menus, she gazed out the front window and studied the dark clouds over the ocean. The waves looked especially rough today. Though it was fun to watch the huge breakers surging toward shore, Maddie shuddered at the sight of people surfing. The California ocean might not be a pitch-black Mississippi lake, but it was still dangerous. With a clear view of the treacherous water, she mindlessly creased each Xeroxed copy of the menu into three parts and watched as stragglers wandered past the restaurant.

Once Halloween passed and the holidays approached, the Fongs saw fewer sit-down customers and mostly relied on take-out orders to sustain the business. Angela was waiting for the state of California to officially recognize her teaching credentials before she could apply for work at one of the local schools, so for now she poured most of her time into making some changes at Royal Palace. She'd added some unique items to the menu that they hoped would translate to an increase in new diners. Along with traditional Chinese entrées with Southern flair, Angela added comfort foods to the dessert menu: key lime pie, peach cobbler, and banana pudding. Besides their usual wine and beer offerings, Royal Palace now served mint juleps, Southern Comfort lemonade, and a special iced tea Angela created called Not Your Mama's Sweet Tea.

Maddie worked fast so she could return to reading *20,000 Leagues Under the Sea,* one of the books she checked out from the school library before winter break started. She also wanted to respond to Brooke's last letter and get it in the mailbox before the last pick-up of the day. Though they didn't write as many letters as they had during the summer, and had only chatted on the phone once this month, Maddie did her best to send Brooke a card or short note whenever she had the chance.

The scent of something savory and hearty drifting from the kitchen caught Maddie's attention. She stacked the menus in a neat pile under the counter and traipsed past the only four diners in the restaurant. Although it was past lunchtime and too early for dinner, these regulars shared a pot of jasmine tea and conversed in Chinese while Popo sat with them and visited.

Maddie swung the kitchen doors open and recognized the scent: Mom's fried chicken and biscuits. The skillets on the stove contained the usual entrées: fried rice, chow mein, and sweet and sour pork. When Maddie peered into the oven, she saw a platter of fried chicken and biscuits—something Mom hadn't made in a long time. When her mother wasn't looking, Maddie slathered a layer of honey butter on a biscuit and took a bite. The butter and honey melted in her mouth. She closed her eyes and smiled, the taste transporting her home to Mississippi.

Before she could sneak a serving of fried chicken, the bell above the front door rang. Maddie dashed to the counter to find a tall, tan, tattooed man in swim trunks and a tank top. She set the rest of the biscuit on a napkin and hid it under the counter. "Hello, welcome to Royal Palace. Would you like a seat? Or are you picking up a to-go order?"

"I was hoping to get some grub. Looks like a good place to eat. Reminds me of back home." The man's voice was deep and soothing. Below his feet a small puddle had formed as water dripped from his board shorts. His bare feet were covered in sand.

"Where's back home?" Maddie glimpsed at the wet floor. Something about the man's dark eyes and bright smile invited her to speak to him. Usually so shy, she rarely instigated any conversation beyond "Enjoy your meal" or "Come back soon."

"I'm from Hawaii, the North Shore of Oahu." The man's well-developed shoulders and biceps were tattooed with patterned, tribal designs, and his skin was tan and smooth. He glanced at the empty tables. "Are you still serving lunch? Or am I too late?"

"No, you're not late. We're open from eleven until ten every day but Sunday. On weekdays, we don't close between lunch and dinner."

Maddie retrieved a menu from the counter and waved an arm to the table nearest the door; then Popo yelled something in Chinese. All Maddie could make out was "feet" or "foot," but the meaning was clear.

"I'm sorry, but my grandmother says you must wear shoes if

you're to eat here."

Popo came storming up to the front and hollered more words and waved her arms. At only four-foot-ten, Popo had a fierce spirit and a raucous voice. She spoke so fast that Maddie could only understand a few words. In Chinese, she asked her to slow down, which only made Popo furrow her brow and march to the kitchen. A couple moments later, Angela came out with Popo trailing behind.

Sweaty and covered in various shades of sauces and gravies, Angela wiped her hands on her apron and greeted the man. "I'm terribly sorry, but my mother doesn't allow barefoot diners in her restaurant."

Popo again yelled at the Hawaiian man and shook her fist. Her voice got louder, and Maddie became increasingly uncomfortable. Relieved her mom was here to handle the situation, Maddie sat atop the stool and pretended to read while she witnessed the transaction between the man and her mother.

"My apologies," the man said. "In Hawaii, we don't often wear shoes, even inside restaurants. I could buy some sandals and come back." He folded his muscular arms and grimaced.

Popo continued to sputter out more angry words in Chinese and approached the doorway. After she muttered something else in Chinese which Maddie didn't understand, Popo opened the door and pointed to the beach.

"She's saying she doesn't want you to bring so much sand into her establishment," Angela said then laughed quietly. "She said a few other things, but they're not worth repeating."

"I understand, no worries. How about I get some chow mein to go and an order of sweet and sour chicken? I can wait outside as the food is prepared. Actually, change the chow mein to *zha jiang mian* and also add an appetizer to my order." He handed the open menu to Angela. "Maybe I oughta get an order of lo mein for later. I've got a pretty big appetite."

"Oh? Just how big?" Angela giggled then covered her mouth with her palm and placed her other hand on the man's buff forearm.

As she ate the rest of the biscuit, Maddie studied her mother's every move, surprised at her giddy behavior toward a stranger, even if he did know how to pronounce *zha jiang mian*.

The man gazed into Angela's eyes for a moment and peered

at the menu in her hands. "What appetizer would you recommend?"

"You can never go wrong with my pork dumplings." Angela leaned against the counter and hugged the menu to her chest.

"Sounds good. I've worked up a pretty good appetite surfing all afternoon. I'm just getting to know the break here at this beach. The water's chilly, but the waves are a lot of fun today."

"Ever since we moved here, I've been trying to get my daughter to swim in the ocean, but she's always got her head in a book. Seems she'd rather do that than enjoy the beach."

"I'm hoping to open a surf shop and school in the spring. Moved here last week to be closer to my parents and figured this might be a good spot to teach surfing. My parents are getting up there in age, so I wanted to be near them. In my culture, we respect our *kupuna*."

"*Kupuna*? Does that refer to one's parents?" There was an odd giddiness in Angela's voice.

"It refers to elders—parents, grandparents, anyone in the community who's elderly. *Kupuna* are very respected in my culture."

"Same with my culture."

By now uninterested in their conversation and only fascinated with Jules Verne's fantastical sea voyage story, Maddie leaned on the counter and began to read, but she paused when her mother laughed once more. Her mother had rarely dated back in Mississippi, yet here she was in California, giggling like a teenager.

"*Kupuna* are revered for their wisdom," the man said, his voice so low Maddie barely heard him. "This is how it is in both Hawaiian and Japanese cultures. Mom is part Hawaiian and Japanese, and Dad is pure Japanese. *Kupuna* often teach the *keiki* important things that modern culture can't do. The elders feel they can teach children much about life."

When he looked at Maddie, she quickly averted her eyes and returned to reading about the giant ship chosen for the journey at sea.

"Since it's just the two of us, we moved into my mother's house with my brother and his family. Southern California is a lot different than Mississippi, but so far, we're enjoying beach life. How about you? Where did you live in Hawaii before you moved here?" Angela asked, her voice high and chipper.

"The North Shore of Oahu," Maddie interjected without looking up from the page.

"It's a small town close to the beach, not as busy as San Clemente, though. By the way, I'm Kai. I think I saw you walking on the beach yesterday morning."

"I walk most mornings before I get to the restaurant. I'm Angela, the main cook at Royal Palace." Angela smiled and stretched out a hand to Kai.

Maddie leaned her elbows on the counter and set her chin in her hands. She skimmed a couple more paragraphs from her book but kept glancing up to observe the unusual way her mother interacted with Kai.

"Nice to meet you, Angela. My real name's Kenny. Kenneth Tamamoto if I'm being formal, but I earned the name Kai after I conquered the huge surf on the North Shore. The word *kai* means ocean in Hawaiian." Kai didn't let go of Angela's hand.

Angela smiled and released her hand from Kai's. "My mother leaves in about twenty minutes. Maybe you can come back in about an hour for a meal you'll never forget. I'll make it worth your wait."

There was a strange smirk on Angela's face. More interested in this bizarre behavior than what happened next in *20,000 Leagues Under the Sea*, Maddie closed the book and focused on every word her mother and Kai said.

"As we surfers say, good things are worth waiting for. There's a Hawaiian word that means to wait for a wave. *Ho'olana*. It's something I learned at a young age. Waiting for a wave taught me patience and how to value something good when it eventually comes my way."

"Good things certainly come to those who wait. I'm fixin' to add a new entrée to the menu. Maybe you'd like to be the first to try it? It'll have a little Southern flair, a couple of surprises for the taste buds. But I'm not sure you have a hankering for Southern food when you came in here expecting sweet and sour chicken and *zha jiang mian*."

"Southern? Now that's got me curious. I'll go rinse off in the shower by the beach and come back later, this time wearing shoes." Kai held Angela's gaze for a moment and smiled—his entire face lighting up. He turned around and left the restaurant.

Angela stood in the doorway and waved as he crossed the

street. Maddie peered over her book and out the window to see Kai strutting along the sidewalk next to the beach with a big black lab at his side. The dog's ebony fur looked so dark against the white sand.

"*Ho'olana,*" Angela said quietly and gazed at the ocean.

Some of the girls at school acted goofy when a guy talked to them, but Maddie had never seen this silly behavior in her own mother. What was so special about guys, anyway?

Angela shut the door and leaned over to hug Maddie. "Honey, I'm gonna freshen up and then return to the kitchen. Keep Popo occupied until Colin gets here to walk her home, okay?"

Maddie nodded and again took in the dark clouds covering the sky. The palm trees bent in the wind, and way out on the ocean, whitecaps formed on the surface. There at the water's edge stood Kai with his dog next to him while the waves crashed on shore. Maddie watched him for a bit before opening her book to where she'd left off. For the first time ever, she was looking forward to the return of a customer.

Chapter Five

San Clemente, California: February 1997

With this being Valentine's Day, Royal Palace was busier than usual. Maddie was sitting next to Ally in a booth as they worked on a DNA project for their science class. Unfortunately, Brian Fluss had also been assigned to her group. Just the sight of him made her stomach churn. While she'd only told Mom and Kai the minimum about Brian, she hoped he'd hate being in the restaurant so much that he'd do his part of the project quickly and leave. Any time she had to look at him, her body tensed, but she did her best to stay focused on the class project.

"Flores, Fluss, Fong," Maddie wrote at the top of the chart.

Ally rifled through the side pouch of her backpack and pulled out a glittery purple pen. "We should start with easy ones like eye and hair color."

Brian snatched the chart from Maddie and glared at her. "How long is this project gonna take?"

"Probably not too long, if we did our tasks at home." Maddie refused to make eye contact with Brian. She opened her textbook to the chapter on hereditary features.

Ally rummaged through her backpack, pulled out two paperbacks, and set them on the table. She searched through her bag until she found a pink spiral notebook and scribbled a few words on the page—the ink a dark maroon with hints of metal. "Oh, I just remembered. I've got a poem to show you." Ally pulled out a thin book with a dark green bookmark sticking out of the middle.

"Another one?" Maddie asked. This was the third time they were studying together and the third poem Ally wanted to show her.

"Yeah. I really think you'll like it." Ally opened the book, removed the bookmark, and pointed to the poem.

Maddie smiled as she read the poem—a short sonnet by a poet named William Wordsworth.

"The bookmark is also for you. I meant to give it to you earlier this week. I got it for you when I was at a cool bookstore in

San Diego last weekend. I thought of you when I saw that quote."

Stoked that Ally thought of her enough to get her a bookmark, Maddie admired the colorful image of a woodsy forest and read the accompanying quote:

May books and nature be their early joy! —William Wordsworth

Maddie smiled and nudged Ally in the shoulder. "Wow, thanks."

"Wordsworth and Coleridge were friends and collaborators." Ally tilted her head and smiled.

Brian waved the chart in front of Maddie's face and tossed it onto the table. "Hey, I don't have all day. I wanna get this stupid project done."

Maddie glared at Brian as she retrieved the chart. "Fine. What color eyes do your parents and siblings have?"

Brian tapped his pencil on the table. "My parents have blue eyes. Well, I think they're blue. Same with my two brothers."

"You don't know what color eyes your parents have?" Maddie gave Brian a disbelieving look, then jotted down "blue" next to his name on the chart and "green" next to Ally's. Besides being the smartest girl in class, Ally had the prettiest green eyes Maddie had ever seen.

Ally leaned her body into Maddie's and studied the chart. She set her elbow on a paperback book, the title obscured by her arm. "My dad has brown eyes, but my mom has green. Like me. But my brother has brown eyes. How about you, Maddie?"

"Brown for my mom, blue for my dad, and brown for me." Maddie recorded the information, even though she had no idea what color eyes her father had. That familiar pang of sadness washed over her when she thought about not having a dad, unlike most kids at school.

But then Ally reached for the chart, and her hand brushed against Maddie's. Warmth filled her insides, displacing the sadness. That happened every time Ally touched her. And each time Ally spoke to Maddie, she looked right into her eyes, causing a fluttery sensation to wash over her. Something about those green eyes made Maddie want to talk to Ally as often as possible.

The door opened and Kai entered, dressed up and holding a

huge bouquet of red roses. Maddie's eyes widened. She'd never seen him in slacks and a button-up shirt. Even his hair was combed, and he wore loafers instead of his usual flip-flops.

Kai had been coming to Royal Palace a few times a week and ate anything Angela prepared for him: lo mein with black eyed peas and okra, fried chicken served over grits with bean curd sauce, and egg foo young with chicken fried steak on top. Fifteen years older than Angela and in his late forties, Kai had a youthful spirit and an appetite as big as his heart. He could also out-paddle and out-surf most of the younger surfers. Maddie often went to the beach after school to watch him surf, but she never went in the water past her knees.

Kai approached the table. "Hey, *keiki*. Your mom here?"

Maddie admired the huge bouquet wrapped in cellophane. "She's in the kitchen with Popo. You should probably wait out here."

Popo's instant dislike for Kai continued over the past couple months, even when he came into the restaurant wearing flip-flops and normal shorts instead of his beach gear. Polite and eager to please Popo, Kai brought her gifts like chocolate covered macadamia nuts or fresh pineapples shipped from Hawaii.

Even covered up in a button-up shirt, Kai's arms looked massive. He leaned over the table and set his palm next to the textbook, which caused Brian to flinch and lean to the side. Kai's muscular body stood out from the people who hung out in San Clemente, but Maddie saw him as nothing but a softy.

"Hereditary traits." Kai used his finger to follow the column in the textbook and grinned. "Dimples, huh? Must've got mine from my dad." Kai scruffed Maddie's hair and returned to the front counter.

Maddie shook her head and laughed. She skimmed the section on dimples and figured she probably got hers from her father. Once she jotted down "dimples" on the chart next to her name, she put a zero next to her mom and an X next to her father. This assignment had to be perfect, and Maddie would make sure Brian's results reflected accuracy, even if she had to alter his findings. She and Ally had both earned the highest scores on the last biology test, but this project would determine if Maddie's grade in the class would bump up to an A.

Ally moved the paperbacks to the far side of the table. "Hair color should be easy. I've got brown, and so do my parents and brother."

Maddie would have to base the answer for her dad on that one photo. "Mine's easy, too. My mom has black hair, my dad has blond, and I've got brown."

"This is stupid." Brian took the wrappers from the straws and crumpled them into small balls and tossed each one into an empty teacup. He repeated this until there were several naked straws strewn across the table.

Ally moved the straws into a neat pile and set the two paperback books on top of her notebook. "Brian, this is due on Monday, so we need to get all our information together now."

Maddie picked up the books and read both titles: *The Rime of the Ancient Mariner and Other Poems* by Samuel Taylor Coleridge and *Flush* by Virginia Woolf. Although she'd read the poem about the ancient mariner, she hadn't read any other poems by Coleridge or anything by Woolf. "Are these books for your English class?"

"My teacher's way into British authors and said we can get extra credit if we do a presentation on an English writer. Coleridge was an interesting and cool poet, but he was deeply troubled. For most of his life he was addicted to drugs. I heard he even wrote some of his poems while he was high."

Brian pounded his fist on the table. "Are we gonna finish this stupid science project or talk about some deeply troubled poet? I don't wanna be here all afternoon."

Maddie ignored his comment as she studied the cover of the book by Woolf. With a cute cocker spaniel displayed on the cover, *Flush* seemed more like something a kid in elementary school would read. Maddie had always assumed that since Ally was in honors English, her reading assignments were more advanced. Surprised an honors English teacher would assign a book about a dog, Maddie was now curious about this author.

Ally leaned into Maddie and flipped the page in the textbook to blood type. "We should move onto the harder hereditary traits. You both got your permission slips signed, right? And the results? Brian, you have your permission slip?"

Brian pulled a crumpled slip of paper from his pocket and handed it to Maddie who smoothed out the form and slipped it into her notebook next to her permission slip.

Angela approached the table and set down a tray with cups and a pot of tea. "How's the project coming along?"

Maddie poured a cup of tea and handed it to Ally. "We're working on the more interesting hereditary trait: blood type."

"When I was a kid, we did that test in class. We got to prick our finger and look at the blood under a microscope."

Ally smiled and took a sip of tea. "It would've been fun to test our blood in class, but the school is pretty strict on classroom safety."

"Well, best to be safe. Let me know if you need anything. I'll bring out some eggrolls in a bit." Angela headed to the front counter and greeted Kai, who kissed her on the cheek and handed her the bouquet.

From the table in the back, Maddie couldn't hear what they talked about, but Angela grinned the entire time she spoke to Kai.

Ally pursed her lips and stared at Brian. "What's your blood type and your parents' type?"

"I'm O-positive, and my mom and dad said they're both A-positive. My older brother is O-positive. I don't know what my little brother is cuz my mom wouldn't let me poke his finger to test his blood."

Surprised that Brian actually tested his blood type, Maddie recorded the results on the chart and checked the textbook—just so she could lean closer to Ally who continued to peruse the section on DNA features.

Angela giggled like a teenager as she led Kai to a nearby table. While Maddie kept her eyes on her mom, she told her classmates about the blood type results. "My mom is O-positive, and I'm B-positive. Since my dad's in Iraq, he of course couldn't provide that information. My mom couldn't remember his blood type."

"It's okay, Maddie." Ally set her hand on Maddie's arm and kept it there while they both continued to look at the charts in the textbook.

That weird fluttery sensation settled in Maddie's stomach. Although she wanted to set her hand on Ally's, Maddie kept her hands on the table while they skimmed the chapter on hereditary features. At school, boys and girls were touchy with each other during lunch or holding hands while they walked in the hallways, but she'd never held a guy's hand, which was fine since she didn't want to have anything to do with boys except to join them in whatever sport they were playing in P.E.

Ally removed her hand from Maddie's arm to take the project sheet from Maddie. "Maddie, since your information is incomplete, we can skip blood type. Mr. Wilkins said we don't have to do every single category."

"You mean I poked my finger for nothing?" Brian tapped his pencil on the table a few times and clinked it on a water glass. "Figures I'd get stuck doing this stupid project with Fajita Flores and Ching Chong Fong."

Maddie felt sick, as she did every time Brian called her that name. But this time she was also angry, and her hands curled into fists. How dare he say that about Ally! Just as Maddie was about to slug Brian, Kai and Angela rushed up to the table.

Kai stepped closer to the table, his arms folded and a stern look on his face. "What did you call them?"

Brian remained slumped in his chair while he tapped his water glass with the pencil. He didn't say a word.

"I said, what did you call these girls?" Kai slapped a hand on the table where Brian sat. "You have two choices right now. You apologize, or I call your parents and tell them about your disrespectful behavior."

Angela set her hands on her hips and glared at Brian. "I oughta call the school and tell the principal about what you said to these girls."

Brian still didn't say anything. He smirked as he pushed the chair back and tapped the pencil on the water glass.

Kai took the pencil from Brian and leaned in close to his face. "You having trouble understanding what we're telling you? If I call your parents, it's not gonna be nice what I tell them."

"Yeah, go ahead. My dad feels the same way about people like them." Brian nodded to Ally and Maddie, then finally looked up at Kai. "And people like you."

"People like what?" Kai looked so angry, like he was going to grab Brian by the collar and drag him out of the restaurant.

"Chinks, Mexicans, you know, people who come here and try to fit in with us."

Angela gasped. "I won't tolerate this kind of behavior in my restaurant. You need to leave right now."

"I'm not Mexican," Ally said quietly, sounding like she was

going to cry. "My dad's Portuguese."

With his arms folded across his chest, Kai looked gargantuan as he towered over Brian. "What about me? You gonna call me a Jap?"

"I'm outta here." Brian grabbed his jacket and stormed out of the restaurant.

Angela set a trembling hand on Maddie's shoulder. "You two are okay now with him no longer here, but if he continues to bother you at school, let us know. I still plan to speak to the principal about his inappropriate comments." Angela gathered the straws from the table and headed to the kitchen.

"Thank you, Mr. Tamamoto," Ally said quietly.

"I bet you girls will get an A plus on this assignment now that he's not here to bother you." Kai winked at Maddie, then returned to the nearby table where Angela approached with a steaming bowl of hot and sour soup.

Now that Brian was gone, Maddie didn't want this study session to end. She wanted to sit here forever with Ally. Maybe they could fill out every single hereditary trait on the chart, even if Maddie had to make up the details about her dad.

Ally moved her hand back to Maddie's arm. "He's right. I bet we'll get an A on this. What other categories should we do? I think we only need three more."

"How about tongue rolling? Both my parents are positive for these traits, and I am as well." Again, Maddie made up the information about her dad, but since she could roll her tongue and so could her mom, her father likely could roll his as well since it was a dominant trait.

"Hey, I've got an idea. Why don't we go to my house to finish this?" Ally beamed when she said this, her smile lighting up her entire face. Noticeably more relaxed now that Brian had left, it was obvious that she too didn't want this study session to end.

"That's a great idea. We still have to type up a report of our findings and use quotes from the book to support our research. I'll pack up some eggrolls and other munchies before we go." Maddie couldn't stop smiling as she packed up her things. Her hands shook as she stuffed her notebook into her backpack.

"We can use the computer in my room and print everything once we're finished. Maybe you can help me pick out some photos for me to turn in for a project in my photography class. We could even sit in the hot tub later if you want."

Ally…in a bathing suit? That strange fluttery feeling got even stronger the more Maddie thought about Ally's green eyes and the way she felt being around her. This would be the best Valentine's Day ever.

Chapter Six

San Clemente, California: June 1997

Now that school was out for summer, Maddie could enjoy more down time. With no homework and lots of free time this week, she thought about writing a fourth letter to Brooke, since there had been no response to the last three. But why bother writing to her if she wasn't going to get a response? Maddie decided to wake up early and go surfing with Kai instead. Over the past few months, Maddie had gone swimming with Ally and also watched Kai surf. Now, she was curious enough to try it for herself.

San Clemente State Beach was quieter than the place by the pier where Maddie usually went, but this seemed ideal for a full day of swimming, surfing, and hanging out. Though several surfers were out in the water, only a few people were on the shore. Maybe the next time Maddie and Ally went to the beach together, they could come here. She'd been hanging out with Ally nearly every day after school for the past few months. They'd become close, especially after Maddie told Ally her dad wasn't fighting in the war and that she'd never even met him. If they weren't studying, they watched a movie or talked until it was time for dinner. Since Maddie now worked at Royal Palace three afternoons a week, sometimes Ally would meet her there and eat dinner together after Maddie's shift.

Maddie sat on the ledge of a fire pit and watched the breakers in the distance, eager but nervous to surf for the first time. Kai hauled the boards from the truck while she sipped hot chocolate from a paper cup. She stared at the soft morning light on the ocean. A few embers, probably left by beachgoers late last night, emitted a bit of heat on her back.

Near the shoreline, small tumblers rolled onto the beach. A few joggers trotted past, and several surfers paddled out to the giant waves. This surf break provided a variety of conditions for all levels of surfers and would be perfect for Maddie's first time. Kai's black Labrador, Kekoa, sat at her feet and nudged her hand to be petted. His name meant "the brave one," and he lived up to it when he would sometimes join Kai on his surfboard. Other times, he was content to lie at Maddie's feet and keep her company while she watched the surfers.

Bundled up in sweats and a hoodie, Maddie read a couple pages from Virginia Woolf's *To the Lighthouse*, one of the books her English teacher recommended as summer reading. She drank the rest of her hot cocoa, tossed the empty cup in the fire pit, and skimmed the next passage:

For now she need not think about anybody. She could be herself, by herself. And that was what now she often felt the need of... To be silent; to be alone...something invisible to others.

Maddie understood exactly what Woolf meant by "something invisible to others." Although content when around Ally, Maddie often was sad and alone at school, especially when other kids teased her for being tall or for being Chinese-American. Not purely Asian and not fully white, Maddie often felt invisible to others.

Since she'd be in tenth grade honors English starting in the fall, Maddie knew she should get a jump on as many classic authors as she could. Especially since Ally also read books by Virginia Woolf.

As Kai approached with two surfboards hoisted over his shoulders, Maddie quickly scanned the next paragraph before they got ready to go in the water:

...and the blue went out of the sea and it rolled in waves of pure lemon which curved and swelled and broke upon the beach and the ecstasy burst in her eyes and waves of pure delight raced over the floor of her mind.

The floor of her mind seemed a peculiar way to describe a person's feelings, but the unique metaphor was surprisingly apt. And Maddie had never heard anyone describe waves as pure lemon. Nearly a third of the way through the book, she still didn't understand all that was happening, but the more she read, the more she became intrigued that words and sentences could be used in such clever and complex ways.

Kai set both surfboards in the sand and rubbed wax on top of Maddie's board. "You ready to hit the waves? The surf report says the water's sixty-five."

Maddie slid her book into her bag. "The water temperature seems warmer than the air right now." She hunched forward and slipped her hands between her thighs to get warm as Kekoa lay over her feet.

"You'll stay plenty warm in that spring suit. The waves are perfect this morning. Just remember what you learned last week about not popping up on your board too soon and be aware that there's lots of reef rock out there which can cut you up real bad if you're not careful."

Maddie studied the waves breaking on shore. That familiar wave of fear washed over her as she recalled that awful night at Clear Springs Lake. But the ocean here was a bright blue, nothing like a dark lake on a Mississippi night. "What if I go under and can't find my way to the surface?"

Kai crouched down next to her and looked at her intently. "I won't let that happen. I'll be close by the entire time."

Maddie's body tensed. "I don't know if I'm ready for this."

"*Keiki*, over the past few weeks, I've seen the way you watch the breaking waves. I had that same look of longing in my eyes when I was your age. The ocean is calling to you. Be silent, and you'll hear the call of the sea."

Maddie observed the steady swell as it headed to shore. "Hopefully I won't wipe out on the first wave."

"If things feel too scary for you, we'll go right back to shore. You did fine in the shallow area when I showed you how to dive under a wave. It's not much different farther out in the water. In fact, it's actually safer because you can gently glide under the breaking wave and not get pounded in the shallow area."

Maddie knew Kai was right. It was time. She nodded and took a deep breath. "Okay, I'm ready to give it a shot." Maddie pulled out the wetsuit Kai bought her last month and set it on the sand.

Kai looped the Velcro around his ankle and then hoisted the board under his arm. Still next to the fire pit, Kekoa sat upright and whined. Even though dogs weren't allowed on this beach, Kai broke that rule because Kekoa always remained in one spot and never ran off.

Maddie took off her sweats and wiggled into her wetsuit. She fastened the leash around her ankle and lifted the board. The surfboard was heavier than she imagined, so she used all her strength to get it snug under her arm and against her hip.

Kai stood next to Maddie and set his hand on her shoulder. "Your mom told me that jerk from school is moving away, said his parents are getting a divorce." Kai shook his head and laughed. "Why would any kid move to Arizona if he had a chance to stay here in Southern California?"

Relieved to no longer have to deal with Brian's taunts, Maddie smirked when she thought of him moving to such a hot and desolate place. "I guess Brian could've stayed here, but he would have had to live in a small apartment with his younger brother and their dad. I heard he'll be living with his mom and grandma in a big house right outside Phoenix."

"Bet you and Ally are glad he's gone."

"Definitely!" Knowing she wouldn't have to see Brian on campus in the new school year only made the summer holiday even better.

They headed to the water's edge, and Kai began to sing a Hawaiian song.

A small wave washed over Maddie's feet. "What's that song called?"

"'*Aia i He'eia*,' an old surfing chant. The song has always been special to me."

The painful memories of Clear Springs Lake arose, but the steady baritone of Kai's voice blended with the wide expanse of the ocean to counter the fear. The memories dissipated, and Maddie felt calm again. "Hopefully the song will bring me good luck as I try to surf. What do the words actually mean?"

Kai furrowed his brow and set his surfboard on the water. "The translation from Hawaiian to English loses some of the meaning, but the words describe the story of King David Kalākaua who tried to impress a woman with his skill at surfing. One part of the song translates to how the waves 'slip and slide, smoothly over the sandbar. It was I who glided all the way to shore, but I was mistaken about finding love there.'"

Maddie grinned. "That's really nice. Hopefully I'll be able to glide all the way to shore."

Kai waded out farther, and Maddie followed him. The cool

water flowed over her feet. Once knee-deep in the ocean, she set the surfboard in the water and glanced back to the dry sand. She was already so far from shore.

For the past several weeks, Kai showed Maddie the proper way to pop up on the board. They practiced in her living room, in his backyard, and on the sand. Kai made her repeat this drill so many times that she had bruises on her knees and on the tops of her feet, but now it was time for her to ride a wave.

"Are we going out to where those surfers are?" Maddie pointed to the area way past the shore breakers.

"In time, *keiki*, but not today. Remember, your mom told me to bring you back safe later today." Kai laughed, his face quickly relaxing into a huge grin.

The surfers soared effortlessly on top of what looked like pretty big waves. None of them looked scared. Maybe Maddie could do it, too. "What if I get up on one of these small waves right away? Then will you take me out to the bigger waves?"

"Maybe in a couple weeks after you master the small ones. This morning, we practice riding waves in the shallow area. Just remember, you never wanna get caught inside."

"Caught inside a wave?"

"No, caught between the shoreline and the crashing waves. Nothing but whitewash in that area. You get caught inside, and you'll have trouble paddling out to the surf line. You end up using up a lot of energy battling the surging water."

An older guy on a longboard paddled up to them and high-fived Kai. "Where you been, dude? Haven't seen you at this break in a few weeks."

"Yo, Jerry! Haven't been here in a long time. Been too busy with the shop and the surf school. Lots of kids wanting to learn how to surf now that it's summer. How you been, bruddah?"

"Busy with surgeries and lots of ortho patients lately." Jerry sat up on his board. "Hey, you hear that Sonny passed away last week?"

Kai shook his head and gazed at the horizon. "I heard the cancer came back. Hadn't seen him out here in a long time. Didn't know he'd passed."

"Sonny stopped treatment last month. He fought a good battle, though. There's a paddle-out Saturday morning by the pier. You two heading to the break outside? The swell's picking up."

Kai steadied Maddie's board and sat upright. "Not today. I'm teaching Maddie how to ride these smaller waves."

"Great spot to teach a kid to surf. Years ago, I brought my son out here for his first time, and now he's on the high school surf team."

Kai looked at Maddie and smiled, his entire face lighting up. "I'd love to see Maddie get on the surf team one day."

"Drew's been wowing the judges at surf competitions. Don't know how he juggles being in the orchestra and in honors classes, but surfing's definitely in his blood."

Kai sifted his hands through the water and looked at the horizon. "The waves are mushy this morning, but that's probably best for Maddie's first time. Less chance of wiping out."

Jerry lay flat on his board and faced toward the line-up. "Yesterday evening things were totally blown out, but things look great now. Well, gotta get out there so I can catch a few waves before my first surgery this morning." He grinned at Maddie. "You got the best teacher here. Did your dad tell you we call him the big Kahuna?"

Before Maddie could correct him, a small tumbler washed over the three of them, and Jerry paddled away. Kai glanced at Maddie and smiled. Maddie had been hanging out at the beach after school since March, and her skin was nearly as dark as Kai's, so it wasn't surprising that this guy thought they were related. This wasn't the first time he'd been mistaken as her father, but neither Maddie nor Kai corrected anyone when they made this assumption.

When another breaker sloshed over her, Maddie steadied her board and studied the huge waves out in the distance. The more they paddled into the surf zone, the bigger the waves looked. She tried to not think too much about that and focused on slicing her hands through the water to make it out to the surf zone.

Already tired from paddling only a few yards, Maddie stopped to rest. "Kai, what's a paddle-out?"

Kai reached his arm over to Maddie's board to steady it. "It's something surfers do to honor a surfer who's passed away. Sonny was a good guy, one of the best old-time surfers here in Southern California. During a paddle-out, a bunch of people paddle past the surf break and form a huge circle in the water. With the surfboards all close together, everyone holds hands. Usually they toss leis and rose petals into the center of the circle as a way to honor the deceased."

"Kinda like a floating funeral?"

"Yeah, pretty much. Once the leis are tossed into the center of the circle, everyone splashes water and cheers."

Maddie had only been to a few funerals, but they were all inside churches or funeral homes. No one ever cheered or tossed flowers to celebrate. The memorials she attended were all somber events. "Seems like a good way to honor the person who's died."

"When I grew up, I learned we should celebrate a person's life and not stay sad for too long after they die. Paddle-outs are common in Hawaii, something we did when a couple of my buddies died while surfing." Kai got quiet and looked off into the distance.

The waves had increased in height, and the hairs rose on the back of Maddie's neck. She grabbed Kai's arm. "Uh, those waves seem like they're getting bigger. Do you ride waves that big?"

"I've mastered much bigger waves on the North Shore of Oahu. Maybe someday you and your mom will come with me to see the big waves of Hawaii. My *ohana* is now your family."

"Thank you," Maddie said quietly. "That'd be fun to meet your family. You think I could ever be good enough to surf huge waves like the ones in Hawaii?"

"Sure, I started out only being able to handle small waves like these. When I was your age, I was nothing but a scrawny kid. Eventually I got good…and got bigger. Next thing I knew, I was surfing Pipeline. I was only fifteen. The guys who'd been surfing most of their life respected me. Well, and I discovered that girls liked surfers."

Even though she'd just turned fifteen, Maddie couldn't imagine surfing huge waves like Kai did at this age. But the floor of Maddie's mind became flooded with excitement. "Do you think I can bring Ally to the beach to watch me surf? I mean, after I get really good?"

"I think you've got what it takes to be a great surfer. Once you get real good, we can have Ally join us here. I'll teach you a few things you can do as you ride the waves to really impress her. Assuming that's what you wanna do…impress this girl, right?" Kai grinned.

Maddie couldn't hold Kai's gaze and quickly glanced into the water. Below the ripples, the pattern of the sand stood out vividly on the floor of the ocean. She never imagined that the ocean was this clear and beautiful past the whitewater.

Kai looked out toward the approaching breakers. "As long as *maka'u* doesn't get in the way, I think you can be good at surfing. I learned as a kid to not let *maka'u* stop me from doing what I love."

"Who's *maka'u*?" Maddie was now used to Kai inserting Hawaiian phrases and names into his conversation, so she tried to learn as many of these words as possible.

"*Maka'u* means fear. In life, you can't ever let fear stop you. You master *maka'u*, and you can conquer anything. These waves are nothing compared to what you might face in life one day. When you catch the first wave of your life, you'll see how amazing it is to surf. No matter where I surf, the first wave of the day is always special." Kai stretched out on his board and paddled toward the breakers, motioning for Maddie to follow him.

Not sure she'd actually stand up on a wave today, Maddie hoped she at least wouldn't wipe out. Once she got settled on her board, she stroked her hands through the water and headed straight for a tumbler. Fear rushed through her body, temporarily immobilizing her. Determined to not let *maka'u* get in the way, she braced herself for the force of the water. The surging wave was very close, but recalling all that Kai taught her, she held her breath and dipped the front of her board under the whitewater. The water gently sloshed over her body. She emerged on the other side of the wave—unscathed and exhilarated. She tilted her head back and laughed as another tumbler headed her way.

Kai was a few feet away and singing "*Aia i He'eia*," his voice so soothing, and Kekoa was patiently awaiting at the shoreline for their return. Once past the breakers, Maddie sat atop her board and ran her hands through the cool water. In her head, she imagined standing up on the wave just like she'd practiced on the sand numerous times.

Kai lay flat on his surfboard and faced toward shore. "Get in position. This looks like a good one for your first wave."

Even though Maddie's hands trembled and her heart thudded hard, she did as Kai taught her and got ready for the wave. When the water formed a crest behind her, she paddled with all her might but couldn't keep up with the momentum of the breaker.

Disappointed that she didn't surf the same wave Kai did, she instead studied how he positioned himself on the board and watched as he surfed all the way to shore.

When a larger wave formed, Maddie got back into position and stroked her hands through the water as the tumbler headed her way. As the wall of water barreled toward her, she somehow pushed away the fear and paddled hard until she tapped into the energy of the wave. For a moment she rode the breaker while lying on her tummy, but then she popped up and got her feet in the right position. Soon, she dipped down the face of the wave and felt in control of the board. How thrilling it was to glide over the ocean—to feel one with the wave.

Maddie rode the tumbler all the way to shore and now understood what Kai meant by how awesome the first wave would be. She waved to Kai from shore, certain he could make out her beaming smile. Eager for a second and a third wave, she paddled through the whitewater and headed toward the cresting waves. As she dove under a breaker, she finally understood Woolf's description of the waves and how "the blue went out of the sea and…rolled in waves of pure lemon." The breakers, tinged with the golden light of morning, surged toward shore while Maddie paddled back to the surf zone.

Chapter Seven

La Jolla, California: January 1999

Maddie had conquered most of the surf breaks in Orange County over the past year and a half, but she'd yet to try surfing at any of the San Diego beaches. In addition to daily surf sessions with Kai or one of the guys from the surf team, Maddie also added weightlifting and running to her training regimen. No longer a lanky young teenager, she'd transitioned into a strong and fit sixteen-year-old who was one of the top competitors on the surf team. She was now ready for a different surf break.

The best place to master larger waves, according to her research, was at a place called Black's Beach in La Jolla, about an hour south of San Clemente. She'd read online that Black's had deep underwater canyons offshore that created more powerful waves and lots of good peaks, which were perfect for a short board. Known as the La Jolla Submarine Canyon, the topography of the ocean floor in this area created a phenomenal surf break but was meant only for advanced surfers.

Maddie also discovered something else: Black's was a clothing optional beach, with mostly naked old men basking in the sun and playing Frisbee or paddleball. With eight- to ten-foot waves predicted at Black's Beach for today, Maddie decided to risk the strong rip currents and the powerful winter swell to hone her skills on the waves. Nothing about the dangerous conditions or the nude sunbathers changed her mind about heading to La Jolla today, especially since Ally agreed to go with her.

In Ally's Jeep Cherokee, they followed the directions to get to the Torrey Pines Gliderport where they would hike down a half-mile trail, which led to Black's Beach. As they cruised down the coast and listened to some hip-hop tunes, they passed Torrey Pines State Beach where Maddie studied the swell out in the distance. They could have parked here and walked to Black's by way of the beach, but that would have been a two-mile walk, and it would likely have been tricky to walk back during high tide. The steep trail down to Black's Beach would be the fastest way to get there.

Once they passed the shoreline, they headed up a road and went past a grove of Torrey pine trees—evidently found only in this area and on an island off the California coast. Maddie caught a glimpse of a sign indicating that the University of California San Diego was half a mile ahead. She lowered the window a couple inches and inhaled the crisp marine air. Excited to spend the day with Ally and to try a new surf break, Maddie felt giddy as they got closer to their destination.

Ally merged into the right lane and pointed to the left. "The buildings along this road belong to UCSD. I went on a tour of the campus a few months ago. Pretty cool location. I'm just not sure they've got the best political science program. UCLA might be better for what I'm looking for."

Maddie shuddered at the thought of Ally going to college in Los Angeles. It was even farther away than San Diego. Whenever Ally brought up where she might attend school in the fall, it was a reminder their time together would soon be extremely limited. Though she hated the idea of Ally moving away and starting college, she knew she should be a supportive friend and appear to be happy for her. "It's cool that UCSD is close to the beach."

Ally bopped her head to the thumping beat of the song on the stereo and tapped her hand on the gear shift. "If I get accepted here and end up living off campus, maybe you could come down to stay once in a while."

The way Ally said "once in a while" sounded so flippant, like she didn't care that they wouldn't see each other all the time and hang out every day. "When do you find out where you got accepted?"

"Probably within the next couple months. If I get accepted to more than one university, I'll have to make a choice about where to go."

"With your high GPA, I bet you'll get accepted to all the schools where you applied."

Ally turned down the music and slowed the car when they neared a stoplight. "Since my brother dropped out of school, my parents are kind of harping on me to pick a prestigious university."

"Didn't your brother get a full ride scholarship to

Northwestern?"

"Not a full ride but close to it. The scholarship covered tuition and books. My parents are pissed that they wasted lots of money paying for Troy's housing and other expenses for him to just end up dropping out."

"I thought he was a good student in high school. Why would he drop out of college?"

"Because he's a fucking loser." At the stoplight, Ally rubbed the back of her neck and stared straight ahead. Usually chipper, right now she was pensive and sullen. "At first, Troy told my parents he hated the weather in Chicago and said the students were snobby. But I think he moved back home because he'd rather get stoned every day and mooch off my parents."

"They're probably now looking to you to be the successful kid, huh? I mean, not that you aren't already."

"Pretty easy to do when I've got a brother who just wants to smoke weed all day and zone out. Ever since Troy moved back home, he seems different. Much more of a loner now."

"Maybe he's depressed?"

"Yeah, could be. Or maybe he's just always high. He's an idiot to have given up such a good thing at Northwestern. Maybe I should apply there. Their application deadline isn't until next month. I've heard they have a really good poli-sci program. Many of their graduates end up getting accepted to the top law schools."

Chicago? That was so far from Southern California. Maddie became quiet and stared out the windshield. With only one semester to go until Ally graduated from high school, she'd been talking so much about where she had applied to go to school: UC Berkeley, UCLA, UCSD, Georgetown, NYU. And now she'd probably add Northwestern to the list. If Ally went to UCSD, at least that wouldn't be too far of a drive from San Clemente.

Maddie hadn't given much thought to where she'd go to college, except that she would likely major in English and stay somewhere along the Southern California coast so she could continue competing. If Ally went to school somewhere close to the coast, maybe Maddie could also get accepted at the same university. But, even though Angela had found a teaching job, they didn't have enough money for Maddie to go to an expensive school like Ally could do.

The sign to the Torrey Pines Gliderport came into view, and Maddie's sadness was put aside for now. Adrenalin pumped in her veins at the thought of surfing down huge peaks and riding through perfect barrels. Ally turned into a dirt parking lot, and they searched for a sign indicating where the trail to Black's started. Huge ruts caused the jeep to bounce up and down as they neared a row of vehicles next to the cliff. A few paragliders were getting ready to launch from the bluff.

Maddie lowered the window all the way and smiled when the surf break came into view. "This surf spot oughta get me ready for the competition after winter break."

Ally slowed the jeep and grinned. "It's been fun seeing you go from a good surfer to one who could compete internationally."

Relieved that Ally was back to her usual chipper self, Maddie shook her head and laughed. "Internationally? I doubt I'm that good. I'll just be happy to place first in the next competition." It was very touching that Ally had noticed how much she'd improved as a surfer, though. They'd spent many afternoons together at the beach after school, and Ally rarely missed a surf competition and always cheered her on. Maddie hadn't realized she'd also been paying such close attention.

Ally smirked as she maneuvered across the deep ruts. "You gonna surf naked?"

Maddie's eyes got big, and her heart thudded hard. "Not in fifty-seven-degree water, but I wouldn't surf naked at Black's even in seventy-five-degree water."

"Might be kinda fun to see you surf naked." Ally's voice was playful and even a bit flirty.

Ally's comment had taken her by surprise, but Maddie remained cool and calm as she thought of how to respond. "If you surfed, you'd understand why it's important to wear a wetsuit or a rash guard to cover important parts of the body like the breasts and…other sensitive areas. I guarantee there will be no naked surfing today…or ever."

Ally gave Maddie another playful look, then pulled into a parking spot. Maddie exited the jeep and stood atop a huge rock to get a better view of the coast. A couple paragliders soared overhead, their red gliders colorful against the bright blue sky. The wind whipped Maddie's hair across her face. Ally stood behind her and took a few photos of the coastline. With the new Nikon she got for Christmas, she'd been taking lots of scenic shots whenever they went to the beach.

Although cold and windy atop the bluff, the sun shone brightly. A thin layer of clouds sat over the ocean far in the distance. With the skies clear overhead, the conditions were perfect for surfing and hanging out at the beach with Ally. They grabbed the rest of their gear from the jeep and headed down the steep trail. The path became treacherous in some parts, so Maddie had to carefully balance over the ridges until she reached a wider part of the trail.

Soon, they made it to the beach and headed closer to what looked to be the best surf spot. As expected, a few nude people were sunbathing and strolling along the shore. Even though the air was only in the low sixties, the nudists basked in the sun—their skin leathery from what'd probably been decades of sunbathing. Though not the type of thing she'd ever do, she wasn't bothered to see beachgoers in the buff, but whenever she passed an old naked guy, she averted her gaze and focused on the ground.

Once they found a secluded spot on the sand, Maddie didn't waste any time getting into her wetsuit while Ally removed her shorts, sweatshirt, and T-shirt and then lay back in her black bikini. Maddie's heart raced when she caught a glimpse of Ally's fit body. In spite of this being the middle of winter, Ally's skin had a beautiful bronze sheen.

Ally ran her fingers through the sand. "What a great way to spend the last day of winter break, especially since it's just us hanging out today."

Just us? Maddie loved the way that sounded, and she couldn't stop smiling. But then she started to worry that Ally would figure out she had a major crush on her, so she busied herself by rifling through her backpack to search for the bar of surf wax. Maddie sometimes wondered if the feelings were mutual, but there'd be no way she'd take things further if she didn't know for sure how Ally felt. Besides, she didn't know the first thing about making the moves on anyone.

Maddie sat on the sand and rubbed some wax on her surfboard. She wanted to stare at Ally's gorgeous body, but she forced herself to look away. "Wish we could have more days like this."

"If I get into UCSD, we could definitely have more days like this." Ally gave Maddie an intimate and flirty look and smiled before rolling onto her tummy.

Her expression just about took Maddie's breath away. The way Ally emphasized the word "definitely" sounded promising and filled Maddie with renewed hope. Maybe Ally also hated the thought of being far from Orange County.

Ally tossed a tube of sunblock to Maddie. "Could you put some sunscreen on my back?"

Maddie kneeled in the sand and smeared a bit of sunscreen on Ally's shoulders and then worked her way down to her lower back. She used slow strokes to make sure Ally's back was sufficiently covered. Maddie gasped quietly as she ran her hands across Ally's back. She'd never imagined her skin would feel this soft.

Maddie capped the sunscreen and handed it to Ally, their fingers momentarily brushing together. The touch of her skin against hers made her heart race. "You mind if I surf for a while? The waves are perfect right now."

Ally rolled onto her side and squinted at the sun overhead as she smiled. "Go for it. Maybe I'll get some good photos of you riding the waves."

Maddie watched the swell far in the distance to figure out where she should enter the water. She looped the leash around her ankle, stepped into the water, and paddled out to the breakers. She dove below a massive wave. The frigid water stung her face. Even though she wore a thick neoprene wetsuit, she still felt the ocean's chill. Another huge tumbler headed her way. Too late to catch it, she dipped below the whitewash. The force of the breaker pushed her to the ocean floor, but she swam through the churning water and emerged on the other side. She hardly ever thought about that awful night in the lake. The frightening moments in the dark water were now a distant memory. Now, huge surf gave her such a rush.

Within a couple minutes, Maddie reached the surf zone and caught a wave right away. She felt the intense power of the breaker as the churning water rumbled under her surfboard. She rode the curl for several seconds but then went aerial and landed on the backside of the wave. The websites that described Black's Beach didn't exaggerate how powerful these waves were, but Maddie was handling them well so far.

One after another, Maddie zipped down the tall face of each breaker and shot through the barrel a few times. These were the biggest waves she'd ever surfed, but she rode them with ease. Kai was right when he told her that a huge wave wasn't much different than a five-footer. A few other surfers sat atop their boards and nodded when they saw Maddie return to the line-up. From what she could tell, she was the only girl out here surfing.

Over the past year or so, Maddie found that guys respected her once they saw her surf. Even her friend Drew Richards, who used to be on the surf team, sought her advice on how to handle big waves. Though he'd asked her out a few times, she always made it clear to him she wasn't into dating and just wanted to be friends.

In between sets, Maddie sifted her hands through the water and looked below the surface to see all the way to the ocean floor. Her feet ached from the cold water. During winter, most of the Southern California surfers Maddie knew wore booties, but she preferred to surf barefoot so she could have better control of her board.

Maddie had drifted several yards north from where Ally sat, so she stroked her hands through the water until she reached another surf break. For a few minutes, she sat atop her board to wait for the next set of waves. She tilted her head back and closed her eyes, enjoying the warm sun on her face.

When her board jostled from a small wave, Maddie got into position and paddled out farther until she reached a cresting wave. Within seconds, she popped up on her board and zoomed down the face. This breaker was the biggest one so far today—at least fifteen feet tall with intense momentum. Maddie grinned as the mist from the wave washed over her face. But, eager to return to Ally, she rode this one all the way to shore.

Amazed that there were hardly any people on the sand, Maddie savored this moment of seclusion. Even in winter, most Orange County beaches were full of people walking or jogging along the shore. Here at Black's, Maddie only saw a few sunbathers far in the distance.

She exited the water and unzipped her wetsuit only to catch a surprising sight on shore: Ally sunbathing topless. Even from a distance, Ally's breasts were gorgeous. Maddie couldn't take her eyes off her, even as she walked across the soft sand, pulled the wetsuit down to her waist, and tightened the straps of her bikini top. When she reached Ally, she peeled off her wetsuit and set it on the sand. Though sunny, the air was chilly yet refreshing.

Ally squinted at Maddie standing above her. "I hope you don't mind. It's not often that I get a chance to sunbathe topless."

Maddie again let her gaze wander over Ally's body. Her breasts were perfect—full, perky, and so beautiful. "I don't mind at all. Hope you don't mind me checking you out." As soon as the words exited her mouth, her cheeks burned, and she wished she'd kept quiet.

"That makes two of us." Ally's eyes traveled from Maddie's face and then down to her midsection and legs.

Not sure what to say, Maddie set her towel next to Ally's and sat down. For over a year now, she'd kept this secret all to herself. Even Kai didn't know the extent of her feelings for Ally. Maddie couldn't ignore the way she felt, yet she also understood it wasn't okay to feel this way about another girl. Though Kai was always supportive and accepting, her mom pushed her to go out with Drew or another guy from the surf team.

After Ally sat up, she scooted closer to Maddie and nudged her shoulder. "I try to not make it obvious when others are around, but I can't help but to look at your amazing body whenever we're at the beach. I've noticed how great you look since you've been working out at the gym and surfing so much."

Maddie couldn't believe what she'd heard. This moment was surreal, but she still wasn't sure how to respond. Maybe Ally meant she appreciated a fit body—no matter the gender. When Maddie went to the gym or the beach, even she noticed both men and women who worked hard to stay in shape.

"Just so you know, even though this is a nude beach, I'm not gonna take off my top." Maddie let out a nervous laugh.

Ally ran her fingers through Maddie's damp hair and then down her back. The touch sent shivers through Maddie's body. The sunlight filtering through Ally's hair made her look even more beautiful than usual. Ally smiled and reached for Maddie's hand. With their fingers interlaced, Maddie now understood that the feelings were indeed mutual. Excited but terrified, Maddie relaxed her body into Ally's—exhilarated to feel skin against skin.

Chapter Eight

San Clemente, California: January 1999

It had been two weeks since Maddie and Ally had held hands at Black's Beach. Maddie wanted to think of Ally as her girlfriend, but they hadn't even kissed. In fact, Ally carried on as if nothing had happened. Had Maddie misunderstood Ally's recent comments and gestures? Should Maddie spend less time with her and find new friends?

That thought flew out of her head the instant Ally called a little while ago, sobbing so hard she could barely speak. She finally managed to say something about Troy being rushed to Mission Hospital in Mission Viejo where she and her parents had been since two in the morning. Home just to shower, feed the dog, and rest, Ally asked Maddie to come over and be with her.

Maddie didn't hesitate. She grabbed her keys and left. Mission Hospital was one of the top trauma centers in Orange County. Troy must be in really bad shape if he'd been admitted there instead of one of the smaller hospitals in San Clemente. Maybe he was hit by a drunk driver? Perhaps he crashed his truck? Maybe he had a brain injury? Or he could possibly have something simple and treatable like appendicitis.

Maddie only barely managed to obey the speed limit in her haste to get to Ally. She sped down empty side streets until she reached Ally's neighborhood. She parked in front of Ally's house, sprinted down the walkway, and knocked on the door. Ally opened it immediately and threw her arms around Maddie, unable to stop trembling.

Maddie held her tight and caressed her hair. "I got here as fast as I could."

Ally pulled away from Maddie's hug and wiped the tears from her cheeks with the back of her hand. "Thanks for coming over. Troy's in really bad shape. He's in the ICU. They've got him on a ventilator."

"A ventilator? What happened?"

"He overdosed."

"Overdosed? On what? I thought you said he just smoked weed."

"The doctors said it was heroin."

"Heroin? Oh, my God." Maddie clasped her hand in Ally's and led her to the couch. She imagined heroin users to be grungy people shooting up in dark alleys or dingy basements. Troy didn't fit that profile at all. "How long has he been using heroin?"

"We don't know. I knew he'd experimented with more than weed, but I never imagined he would try heroin. Last night at around midnight, he was in his room with the TV up really loud. I yelled through the door to tell him to turn it off, but he didn't respond. I just figured he was in a deep sleep, but I was really pissed he wouldn't turn off the TV. After a while, I finally opened his door and turned it off. Then I noticed he didn't look right. I tried to wake him up, but he was unresponsive." Ally started to cry again.

Maddie put her arm around her. "How horrible that must've been to see your brother that way. They're sure it was a heroin overdose?"

Ally rested her head on Maddie's shoulder and let out a loud sigh. "The paramedics saw track marks on his legs."

"Where you and your parents wouldn't have noticed." Maddie shook her head and caught sight of a framed family portrait on the fireplace mantel. She'd always seen the Flores family as being so balanced and happy, as exemplified in this photo, but she also understood that many families had buried secrets and issues. People were at least sympathetic to learning Maddie lost a father in the war. They wouldn't be as kind to a family dealing with addiction.

"This all feels so unreal to me, but it's all starting to make sense." Ally shook her head and let out a sob. "I mean, as far as why Troy has changed so much these past few weeks. Just now I searched through his room and found a couple pipes and a joint and some syringes. Also found some pills. Maybe ecstasy or speed. There's no telling how long he's been using heroin. The overdose could have even been caused by him unknowingly smoking what he thought to be weed which was tainted with heroin, or he could've been buying heroin and shooting it up for weeks now. There's no way for us to know for sure until he wakes up...if he wakes up."

"This is all so unbelievable."

"The paramedics gave him something called naloxone. I guess this drug blocks the effects of heroin if administered soon enough, but the doctors in ICU aren't sure if they gave him this drug in time to stop any significant damage."

Everything Ally said sounded like a strange dream and seemed similar to something on a reality cop show. "Where would he have bought heroin?"

"I don't know, but I guess at this point it doesn't matter. If he survives, my parents will put him in rehab right away."

This was all so far out of Maddie's experience. She'd never had drugs or alcohol, excluding a few sips of plum wine on Thanksgiving, Christmas, and Chinese New Year, which wasn't even enough to get tipsy. "My God, I'm so sorry." Maddie held Ally tighter.

"I know I often say that Troy's a jerk, but…he's my brother. I've always seen him as such a loser, but I don't want to lose him."

"He's in one of the best hospitals in Orange County." Maddie wanted to comfort Ally, but she knew nothing she said could ease her fears right now, so she fell silent.

When the phone rang, both of them jumped. Ally dashed to the kitchen to answer the call. Maddie waited in the living room with the fluffy mutt next to her. Cooper was some sort of beige terrier mix and usually followed Ally everywhere. Not only did he remain on the couch this time, he allowed Maddie to lift him onto her lap and rub his belly. While Ally continued her call, Maddie absentmindedly pet Cooper and mulled over all that'd transpired over the past couple weeks: the awareness that Ally was also interested in her, the sensation of how amazing it felt to have her hand clasped in hers, the desperation in Ally's voice when she asked Maddie to drive over here tonight. Although naïve in all relationship matters, these sorts of things certainly seemed to describe someone with girlfriend status.

Cooper jumped off her lap and dashed toward the kitchen. Maddie looked up to see Ally gripping the back of a dining room chair and crying. She rushed to Ally's side and pulled her into her arms.

"He woke up," Ally said between sobs. She didn't pull away from Maddie's embrace. "He hasn't spoken, but he's communicating in how he blinks and squeezes my mom's hand. His vitals are more stable now."

"Oh, thank God. Maybe we should drive to Mission Hospital. We could be there in minutes. I bet my mom and Kai would meet us there. Maybe we can bring your parents something from Royal Palace, like some egg drop soup or low mein. They're open for another hour."

Ally pulled away from Maddie's hug and dabbed her eyes with a tissue. "Thanks, but my parents already ate. They told me I should stay home because there's not much I can do at the hospital. My mom's gonna stay the night at the hospital, but my dad will be home in a few hours. Part of me wants to just sneak in to see Troy, but I know it'll just stress my parents even more."

Maddie slipped her hand in Ally's. "Whatever you need, I'm here."

Ally bit her lower lip, her eyes focused on the marble floor. "There's no way I can go to school tomorrow. I just want to sleep late, maybe soak in the hot tub before I head to the hospital. The doctors say Troy will improve over time, but I think it'd be okay if I go to the hospital a bit later in the day. Will you stay here tonight? I'm so tired, but I don't want to be alone."

"Of course. I'm not going anywhere." Maddie wiped a tear from Ally's cheek. She wanted nothing more than to take Ally into her arms and hold her all night long. She also wanted to kiss her, but this wasn't the right time.

Maddie made a quick call to tell her mom she was staying the night at Ally's. Not only did her mother understand that her friend needed support right now, she said Maddie could take the next day off school if Ally needed her.

After Ally flipped on the porch light and turned off the lamp in the living room, they headed upstairs to Ally's room. Cooper trotted close behind and hopped on her bed; he curled up in a ball atop a crocheted blanket. Though Maddie had been here many times when they studied together, tonight would be different. There'd be no notebooks strewn across the comforter, no textbooks forming a barrier between their bodies on the bed.

Ally clicked on the bedside lamp, plopped on the bed, and unlaced her sneakers. Maddie stepped out of her flip-flops and sat at the foot of the bed. When Ally lay back and stared at the ceiling, Maddie snuggled next to her.

Ally wrapped an arm around Maddie and pulled her closer. "Thanks for being here tonight. I can't imagine going through this without you."

"I'll be here for as long as you need me." Maddie set her head on Ally's chest and closed her eyes. Through the thin T-shirt, Maddie heard the steady beat of Ally's heart. The simple thud of her heartbeat made everything seem totally fine right now.

Ally ran her fingers along Maddie's ribcage and rested her hand on her hip. "I keep seeing Troy's unresponsive body flashing in my head. It's just so…fucking awful. When I nudged his shoulder and he didn't move, I thought he was dead. I wish I would've gone in his room earlier. I could've stopped him from overdosing."

Maddie sat upright and propped herself up on her elbow. She stuffed a pillow under her arm and looked at Ally intently. "I don't think you could have stopped him from overdosing or even prevented him from using such dangerous drugs, but you probably saved his life by going into his room and noticing he was unconscious." Maddie set her hand on Ally's cheek then moved it to her chest. Through the T-shirt, Maddie felt Ally's heart thudding hard.

Without saying a word, Ally reached under her T-shirt and removed her bra and got under the covers. Likewise, Maddie took off her bra, crawled under the sheets, and spooned her body behind Ally's. She ran her hand down Ally's hip and thigh. Even through thick sweats, Maddie could feel Ally's firm muscles. For a few moments, they lay quietly as Ally now seemed calmer.

But after a couple minutes, Ally flipped over and moved closer. The intensity in her eyes was surprising. She stared at Maddie as she ran her fingers through Maddie's hair. "This wasn't how I imagined our first kiss."

"Oh, yeah, me neither." Maddie laughed and averted her eyes from Ally's as she squirmed under the sheets.

Ally narrowed her eyes and smiled. "You've never kissed anyone, have you?" She sounded surprised yet excited.

"Is it that obvious?" Maddie giggled and buried her face in Ally's neck.

Ally moaned softly and ran her fingers down Maddie's arm. "I love that I'm the first person to kiss you. There's something so sweet about a first kiss. Well, about any kiss, for that matter. How long have you been wanting to kiss me?"

Ally's question sent a surge of electricity through Maddie's body, but the comments about kissing seemed so loaded, as if Ally must have kissed a few people. Or more than a few. Though she'd dreamed about kissing Ally for months now, Maddie worried she wouldn't be good enough.

"Maybe as long as you've been wanting to kiss me," Maddie finally said, shocked at her boldness. Though her heart thudded hard, she relaxed her body into Ally's. Here to comfort Ally and help her cope with her brother's situation, Maddie would do everything she could to keep her mind off things, even if it meant making out for a while before they drifted off to sleep.

As Ally ran her hands through Maddie's hair, she kissed her softly on the lips. The kiss sent shivers through Maddie's body. Eager for Ally's soft lips, Maddie kissed her again. The kisses quickly became more intense. Maddie couldn't get enough. She reached under Ally's shirt and ran her fingers over her lower back. Ally kissed her even harder and pulled her closer. Ally's lips and tongue awakened a part of Maddie she'd never known was there.

After they made out for a while, they snuggled under the soft sheets. Ally yawned, and her eyes got heavy. Though she wanted to feel Ally's lips on hers once more before drifting off to sleep, Maddie was satisfied for now. When Ally fell asleep, Maddie wrapped her arms around her and held her tight. Hopeful that Troy would be okay, Maddie knew she would be there for Ally no matter what. She was elated that she and Ally had taken things a step further, but she was tired and should get some sleep. They had tomorrow morning to hang out. And many more days beyond that.

Chapter **Nine**

"Quiksilver wants to sponsor you?" Ally gave Maddie a quick hug and pulled away to rummage through her locker. "How'd they discover you? Aren't they one of the top surf companies in the country? This is amazing!"

The building was louder than usual since this was the last day of classes before spring break. Students spilled out of classrooms and into the hallway, their chatter accentuated by an occasional giggle or locker slam.

Maddie leaned against the locker next to Ally's and nodded to a couple girls from the surf team. "I don't think it's definite yet, but I guess some of the Quiksilver reps have been going to the local surf competitions and noticed me. Also, someone saw the photos you took at my last competition."

Ally peeked around the door of her locker, and her eyes widened. She shook her head and laughed. "No way! The ones from the school newspaper? My photos helped to get you this offer? I had no idea someone from Quiksilver would even notice those."

"For now, they want some headshots and more photos of me in the water. I'm not sure to what extent they'll sponsor me. It might just be that they want to represent me as a junior surfer until I graduate from high school and then see how I do."

"I think we should get some photos of you in your bikini." Ally smiled and peered down the hallway where swarms of students hovered around their lockers. She leaned closer and quietly said, "Maybe we can do a photo shoot at Black's Beach next week. Besides, I need to work on my senior project for my photography class. I've got plenty of scenic shots, but I need way more action photos and headshots. Black's seems perfect as far as surfing photos." Her voice became low and sultry. "And maybe some other poses."

For the past two months, Maddie hadn't stopped fantasizing about seeing Ally topless at the beach. "Sounds like a perfect spring break. Kai wants me to do some intense training this weekend, but after that, my week is pretty open. What if we do a few photos at my house this afternoon…in my room? Mom and Kai won't be home until late."

Ally's response was a wicked smile, which was definitely a yes to Maddie's suggestion. Maddie walked across the hallway to her locker. After she opened it, she found someone had slipped an envelope inside. She recognized Ally's handwriting on the front: "Open when no one is around…xoxo."

In the upper left-hand corner was a tiny heart in red ink. Maddie glanced behind her to see Ally smiling at her.

There was no way she could wait until later to see what Ally had written, so she took a quick peek inside the envelope:

Even though we just saw each other a few hours ago, I can't wait to see you again. I never imagined that kissing someone could be—

Maddie's hands trembled as she quickly stuffed the note into the envelope. When three girls from the track team wandered past and said hi, Maddie slipped the envelope into her backpack and pulled her letterman jacket out of her locker. Though warm inside the building, she put it on anyway and rummaged through her locker to figure out what she should bring home for spring break. As she thought about what Ally said in that note, her heart thudded hard. She couldn't wait to be alone with Ally.

Maddie grabbed a couple copies of *Surfer* magazine and slipped them into her backpack. Maybe they could get ideas on how best to photograph Maddie at the beach and in the water. She also grabbed the bathing suits and board shorts she always kept in her locker whenever she wanted to go right to the beach after school.

"Hey, congratulations," Drew said from behind her. "Coach just told me the news. With Quiksilver as your sponsor, I bet you'll get tons of cool gear. Maybe you'll even get to meet Laird Hamilton and Kelly Slater."

Maddie gave Drew a brief hug. "I doubt I'll meet anyone that big. They're not gonna want to meet some sixteen-year-old surfer girl."

"You never know. They were younger than that when they started to get noticed."

Maddie took in Drew's dressy attire and polished shoes. "Are you on your way to an interview or something? What's with the collared shirt and slacks? Is that how students dress at Chapman?"

Amidst a crowd of kids in T-shirts and jeans, Drew looked nerdy in his button-up shirt and slacks, but in a sweet way he looked handsome. Tan and clean-cut, Drew kept his sun-bleached hair buzzed short and didn't dress in typical surfer clothes. "I was talking to the principal at the nearby elementary school about possibly doing some volunteer work with the kids. Maybe develop some sort of music program."

"You should talk to my mom at her school. She'd probably be open to you doing something with her class." Though her mom was still new at the elementary school where she taught, she'd already made lots of new connections with the other teachers.

"I figure working with the kids will help me decide if I want to get into teaching. My dad's still pushing me to go to med school. But, for now I'll just focus on finishing up at Chapman."

"I think it'd be pretty cool to teach. Coach wants me to help out on the surf team after I graduate, maybe even be the assistant coach, but Kai is pushing me to train and qualify for the U.S. Open of Surfing for next summer since I'll be eighteen by then. Not sure I can do both because the training would be pretty intense."

"That'd be cool if you're an assistant coach, especially if you go to school somewhere in Orange County. Chapman's not that far from the beach."

Now a music and biology major at Chapman University, as well as a member of the school's orchestra, Drew took his studies seriously and had remained in contact with Maddie after he graduated. All throughout high school, he was the best surfer on the men's team, but he was never like the other guys. Always attentive when they chatted, Drew listened whenever Maddie went on about her surf competitions. There was a sweetness about him that other guys didn't have.

"Not sure Kai and my mom can afford Chapman, even if I get a scholarship. I'll probably end up going to Saddleback for two years and then transferring to Cal State Fullerton."

Even though Angela made decent money from her teaching job and worked at Royal Palace on the weekends to help supplement her income, they didn't have an abundance of money to pay for Maddie to go to a private university. Being sponsored by Quiksilver didn't necessarily mean Maddie would make enough money to pay for college; at best, she'd get a lot of cool clothes, a couple new surfboards, and some wetsuits. The local community college seemed the best option for her.

Maddie stuffed her literature textbook into her backpack but left the math and science books in her locker. Across the hall, Ally chatted with one of the players from the basketball team. Maddie narrowed her eyes. That was the guy who'd asked her to winter formal. Ally had turned him down and instead went to the dance with Maddie and a bunch of their friends, a relief at the time, but why was she talking to him now? Ally laughed at something the basketball player said, and Maddie slammed her locker shut.

"Maddie, I'll meet you in the parking lot," Ally called out, then headed down the hall with the guy.

Drew leaned against the lockers and folded his arms as he studied the floor. "So, you wanna go to T-Street with me? I hear the swell is pretty good right now. Maybe later we could get fish tacos at Rubio's, and you can tell me more about this awesome Quiksilver offer."

"No, I gotta get going."

"That's cool, but maybe we can surf next week since it's spring break. It'd be fun to try some of the surf breaks in San Diego."

"Actually, I'll be pretty busy next week since Mom and I are moving into Kai's house."

"With his parents?"

"They're actually pretty cool, and the house is huge. I finally get my own room. Maybe you can meet me at Trestles on Saturday or Sunday. That's where I'll be with Kai for the next two days. He's gonna have me try out a couple different boards from his shop."

"Sounds good, I'll give you a call." Drew waved goodbye and went on his way.

Maddie hoisted her backpack over her shoulder and met Ally at her jeep. There was no sign of the basketball player. Good. Then spring break was off to a great start. The reprieve from daily classes was also very welcome, even if she did have some assigned reading to do.

They drove out of the school parking lot and were two blocks from the school when Ally reached for Maddie's hand. "Let's go to my house instead. If we're gonna get some photos of you, I'd need to stop there anyway to get my camera."

"Didn't Troy just get home from rehab? I'm guessing your mom is watching him closely since he hasn't been sober for too long."

"He's been in a clean-living facility for thirty days, maybe more. He was only home for two days before my mom found a place that could take him. Right now, she's hanging out with my aunt, and my dad's at work. So, there's no one home." There was a playfulness in Ally's voice, a tone Maddie loved hearing.

"I've got a couple bathing suits in my backpack, including the blue one you love so much."

"Let's do the headshots once I get my better lens. For now, I'll get some shots of you in your royal blue bikini. We could do some photos of you in the backyard since my parents won't be home until seven or so. Maybe I'll get a few of you as you're getting out of the pool."

As they drove along the coast, Ally told Maddie more about Troy's rehab. "We have to attend weekly family therapy sessions, and the counselor suggested a few one-on-one appointments for each of us."

Ally seemed tense as she talked about all of this. But at the stoplight, she looked at Maddie and smiled as she squeezed her hand. Maddie loved that right now they carried on like a normal couple.

"I love how our hands fit so well together." Maddie pulled Ally's hand to her lips and kissed each knuckle. Maddie's heartbeat sped up as she worked up the nerve to talk about an important topic—something she'd been wanting to say for a couple weeks. "I was thinking…it'd be neat to go to your prom with you."

"You mean, as my date?" Ally laughed.

"Why not? We went as part of a group to winter formal. But maybe it's time we went to a dance together."

"Maddie, you know I love hanging out with you." Ally let go of Maddie's hand and gripped the steering wheel. "It's just that…I'm not okay with anyone knowing about us."

"Ever?" Maddie stared at her hands loosely clasped in her lap.

"For now, I like how things are with us." Ally looked at

Maddie and set her hand on her thigh. "I actually like that it's our own little secret. Makes it more special."

Maddie's heart continued to thud hard. The feel of Ally's hand on her leg sent shivers through her body. "Yeah, I get it," Maddie said quietly. Though disappointed that Ally wouldn't go to prom with her, Maddie did her best to shake it off and focus on this moment. She set her hand atop Ally's and thought about how fun their photo shoot would be.

Once they got to Ally's house, Maddie changed into her bathing suit and grabbed the surfing magazines from her backpack and headed outside. Cooper pranced over to her, and Maddie greeted him with a back scratch and cuddle. Though she'd never been in the Flores's pool, she'd hung out on the patio a few times. The black-bottomed pool and the stone waterfall at the far end made the backyard look like an oasis.

With Diet Cokes in hand, they sat at the edge of the pool and dangled their feet in the water as they flipped through the magazines for photo ideas. The plum-colored polish on Ally's toes contrasted with the dark water in the pool.

"What about these?" Maddie pointed to a series of photos— the silhouette of a surfer sitting atop his board at sunset, one of him riding through the curl of a wave, and another image of him standing on shore.

Ally leaned close to Maddie and studied the photos for a moment. She always became pensive when looking at a photo or reading a piece of literature. Ally handed the opened magazine to Maddie and scanned the pool and yard. "Let's get some images that'll show off your body but also convey how awesome you are on the waves. Like the one of the surfer in this photo spread. I mean, look at his amazing chest and shoulders. The way he's standing next to that cabana while looking at the crashing waves is pretty hot."

He was? Not to Maddie. Why would Ally say that? Maddie decided to ignore the comment. "The surfers always look grungy in these magazines. From what I've noticed, it seems like these types of photos are suggesting surfers aren't motivated to do anything but surf."

"Well, pro surfers might not make great boyfriends, but they sure do have sexy physiques. That's exactly what we need to convey in your photos. We might as well get you looking as hot as we can in these photos." Ally unzipped a small pouch and removed some lipstick and mascara. After she examined Maddie's hair and face, she handed her a compact mirror and the tube of mascara.

Although Maddie rarely wore make-up, a little bit would enhance her features. "You do realize that when and if Quiksilver does sponsor me, it'll be this summer when I'm seventeen. I'm not sure at this point that my photos should look sexy."

"I know…but we might as well do some photos for our eyes only—ones that won't be used for my senior project. I'll be sure to develop them in the darkroom at school when no one's around." Ally smiled and reached over to brush the hair off Maddie's shoulder. "You ready for this? I might sound bossy at times, but I just wanna make sure I get the right shots before the sun goes down."

"I don't mind bossy," Maddie said with a quiet laugh. "Just tell me where you want me."

"Wait right here for now." Ally clomped across the wooden deck and retrieved a canvas satchel from the table. She searched through the bag with such an intense look on her face, as if she'd already envisioned a full photo shoot with various poses and outfits. "I've got some other ideas I'd like to try before we do the bikini shots. We'll first do some photos with you in this." Ally pulled out a sheer white shirt and handed it to Maddie.

Maddie looked it over and wondered what Ally had in mind for the first few photos. "You want me in just this?"

"For now, keep your bikini on." Ally smirked and handed her the tube of lipstick.

"What exactly am I wearing?" Maddie slipped the white shirt over her bathing suit and buttoned it all the way to the top. The material went a few inches below her bikini bottoms, but it was so sheer she could see her tan skin through the material. Maddie put on a layer of lipstick and smeared her lips together. Not accustomed to wearing anything but lip balm, her lips felt unpleasantly sticky.

Ally stood inches from Maddie's face while she used her finger to blend in the lipstick. "It's my mom's cover-up when she's sitting by the pool when others are around. She thinks the blouse covers her body, but as you can see, it's totally sheer. Wow, it looks amazing on you, and that lipstick is a perfect color with your skin tone. Why don't you stand over there, by the white roses? We'll start with something a little sweet and innocent."

Ally set the camera on a redwood bench next to the flower-bed. She reached over to fluff up Maddie's hair and adjust the cover-up. Ally straightened the collar and fumbled with the top of the blouse. First, she unbuttoned one button. Then another. Soon, the entire front was opened to reveal Maddie's blue bathing suit top and the subtle hint of cleavage. With Ally's hands so close to her breasts, Maddie felt the heat surging inside her. Since she knew this wasn't the right moment to suggest they finally take things further, Maddie kept her hands to her sides, but she hoped this photo shoot would lead to time together in Ally's bedroom later.

Ally stood a few feet away and focused the camera. "Move to the right a little. I wanna get the right ratio of sky, ocean, and flowers behind you in these shots. Take one more step to the right, but only about six or seven inches."

Maddie felt awkward and stiff until Ally came over and angled her body so that the photo would capture her side view. Nearby, Cooper burrowed his snout in the flowerbed. When Ally set both hands on Maddie's hips to adjust her body, it sent an intense surge of warmth through her. Maddie resisted the urge to kiss Ally—for fear she'd smear the lipstick or ruin the position of her body for the photo.

"If this is you being bossy, I like it." Maddie looked deep into Ally's eyes and laughed.

Ally smirked and adjusted Maddie's hair so that it cascaded down her back and over her shoulders. "You just wait until we do the close-ups."

"Or the photos for our eyes only." Maddie smiled.

Ally took a few photos at various angles then gave the pool a calculated look. "I think we should do some photos of you in the pool before sunset. With the black-bottomed pool, I bet I can make the photos look like you're in the ocean at dusk. The light-ing is perfect right now. Once you get in, stand where you're just waist-deep. I'll get some of you sifting your hands through the water and maybe a couple of you floating on your back."

Maddie slipped out of the sheer cover-up, stepped into the pool, and waited for more instructions from Ally. Though the water was at least eighty degrees, the air had become chilly now that the sun sat lower in the horizon. When Ally too entered the pool, Maddie immediately imagined them making out. But to her disappointment, Ally remained at the steps as she took a few photos.

"Okay, take another couple steps deeper but don't get your hair wet yet." Ally stood at the side of the pool and took a few more photos. "Perfect, now dip below the water and emerge over here where I'm standing."

Still in the shallow end, Maddie submerged under the water and did exactly what Ally suggested. She'd never been part of a photo shoot before, other than the group photos for the surf team, but this all seemed professional—and also incredibly exciting and erotic.

Ally met Maddie at the shallow end where she held out a towel for her. "Here, dry off a bit, and I'll take a few more photos of you by the side of the pool. With the amber rays of light streaming through the clouds, let's get a couple more of you with the ocean in the background. I don't usually like silhouette images, but let's do a couple anyway."

"After you take those photos, why don't you join me in the pool?"

"Let's just focus on these shots before we lose the good lighting."

Maddie dropped the towel onto the deck and stepped back into the pool. "I'm not a photographer, but I think I know enough to realize we lost the good lighting a while ago."

"Maddie, come on." Ally picked up the towel and held it out toward Maddie.

An intense yearning flooded through Maddie's body. "We've got all of next week to get some actual ocean shots with me in my bikini and on my surfboard."

"How are we to know there won't be a ton of people at Black's Beach next week? Most schools will be on spring break."

Maddie swam to the ledge of the pool. "Ally, relax. Come in the pool with me. We're the only ones here right now. Just let yourself go for once. I think we got some good photos already. Let's enjoy this moment together before your parents get home."

To Maddie's surprise, Ally set her camera on the patio table and stepped into the pool. Fully clothed, Ally swam toward Maddie and kissed her softly on the lips. Maddie giggled when she thought about the absurdity of Ally in the pool while in her shorts and T-shirt, but their kisses quickly became passionate. Ally's lips and tongue were soft and eager.

When they embraced, Maddie felt Ally's hard nipples through her wet T-shirt and sports bra. The burning in her stomach was calm compared to the torture of the restricting clothes that covered Ally's body. Though never open to being nude around others, Maddie wanted to slip out of her bathing suit and press her naked body against Ally's, but she resisted this urge.

Maddie pulled back and gazed at Ally in the golden light of sunset. As she cupped her hands around Ally's face, she kissed her softly on the lips. Ally removed her wet T-shirt and tossed it onto the deck. Maddie set her hands atop Ally's sports bra and felt her full breasts and erect nipples. How amazing those hard nipples felt under Maddie's hands. When Maddie's hands roamed lower, Ally halted the progression and moved them back to her chest.

The shadows from the setting sun and the dim lights in the yard highlighted Ally's green eyes and full lips. Once again, Maddie pressed her lips against Ally's. When Ally moaned softly, Maddie kissed her harder. A heat radiated through her body and settled between her legs.

Maddie set her hands on Ally's hips. "I've been wanting to kiss you all day."

"That makes two of us." Ally wrapped her arms around Maddie's body and kissed her again.

Maddie pulled back for a moment—her breath shallow and shaky. She looked deep into Ally's eyes and smiled. There was a softness about Ally's beauty, yet the way she kissed her also showed a passionate fire that burned hot. The tickle of Ally's damp hair on Maddie's shoulder got her even more turned on, but when she recognized the hesitation in Ally's eyes, Maddie pulled her closer and kissed her softly on the neck but didn't take things further.

When she realized she shouldn't rush things, Maddie led Ally to the edge of the pool where she held her in her arms. She'd never felt so satisfied and happy as she did right now, but she understood they'd need to take things at a much slower pace. Ally's sweet kisses showed Maddie that she too wanted to be together. Maybe not tonight but eventually.

Chapter Ten

Del Mar, California: June 1999

In the small compartment of the Alpine Bobsled ride, Maddie and Ally squealed when the ride operator increased the speed. While loud music thudded from the speakers overhead, Maddie gripped the metal safety bar as the ride went around at dizzying speeds. When the bobsleds went faster, Maddie set her hand atop Ally's. Everyone screamed when the velocity increased even more. Maddie hadn't stopped grinning since she'd climbed into the cramped sled. Though they'd gone on a couple other rides this afternoon, the Alpine Bobsled ride was the best one so far—since they had to sit close together.

With Ally's body squished next to hers, Maddie didn't want this moment, or the day, to end. As the bobsleds continued to zoom in circles, her face hurt from laughing so much. Other rides and exhibits in the fun zone blurred past as the sleds went even faster. Maddie heard Ally giggling, which made her laugh even harder.

Not sure she could take much more of the bobsled ride, Maddie did her best to focus on the metal bar and not let the dizziness get to her. They still had a few more hours to enjoy the Del Mar Fair before they headed back to Orange County. How pathetic it would be for Maddie to be sidelined due to queasiness from a silly bobsled ride. As the speed gradually decreased, Ally set her hand on Maddie's thigh just below the hem of her shorts. The gesture surprised Maddie but also excited her. But when the ride slowed to a complete stop, Ally moved her hands to her lap.

Maddie's heart was still pounding hard as they exited the ride and tromped down the metal stairs. She took a few deep and slow breaths and scanned the crowd—her eyes settling on Ally. So cute in her tight denim shorts, she'd become even hotter these past few months since she'd gotten into running and cycling. The best part of being at the Del Mar Fair was that Maddie got to spend the entire day with Ally at her side. Plus, soon she'd get to see Ally's photojournalism piece, which she entered to the fair a few weeks ago.

Days like this made Maddie feel less sad about Ally moving to L.A. in seven weeks. While Maddie would experience her last year of high school starting in the fall, Ally would begin her first semester at UCLA as a political science major. Although Ally would only be about an hour and a half away and would likely come home a couple times a month, Maddie hated the thought that they would no longer be in the same city.

Maddie grimaced and pulled her hair out of the ponytail, then sat on a bench near the bobsled ride. "I think I need a break from the fast rides."

"Maybe we need something a little more mellow, like a stroll through the goat exhibit." Ally laughed and plopped down next to Maddie. Less stressed about Troy now that he'd been in a sober living home for three months, Ally had returned to her usual jovial self and was clearly enjoying her time at the fair.

Maddie smiled and relaxed her body into Ally's. A guy and girl walked past with their arms around each other. Another couple wandered by, hand-in-hand. Though happy to spend the day with Ally, Maddie wished she could hold her hand or wrap her arm around her as they checked out the exhibits or played one of the carnival games.

They left the bench and strolled past the loud and chaotic games. Maddie watched more fairgoers play carnival games. "How about we go see your photojournalism piece? I think the photo exhibit is right around the corner from the fun zone."

"No, not yet. Let's do that last. What I entered is sort of a surprise for you." Ally smiled and nudged Maddie's shoulder. "Something I'd like to save for later."

"A surprise? What have you been up to?" Maddie cocked her head.

"You'll see." Ally gave Maddie a cheeky grin. "All I'm gonna tell you is that they're photos I took over the past year and that I won a blue ribbon." Her fingers brushed against Maddie's for a quick second. Ally always kept her hands to herself whenever others were around, but in private she was always cuddly and sweet.

While they passed through the fun zone, Maddie watched foolish fairgoers waste their money on carnival games. A bunch of young guys stood next to a booth and attempted to toss ping pong balls into small fish bowls. Any time one of them actually made a successful shot, the others hooted and whacked the guy on the back. When Ally slowed down to watch them play the game, Maddie stood behind her but was bothered they hadn't left the fun zone yet.

Determined to convince Ally not to waste her money, Maddie leaned close and said, "Most of these games are rigged. You'd have better luck with the water gun game over there." Though she hadn't been to a county fair since she lived in Mississippi, she recalled how the majority of these games were set up to not have too many winners.

Ally didn't respond but kept looking at the young men, most of whom looked like frat boys and partiers. They all wore tight T-shirts that showed off their buff bodies.

"Dude, you should be good at this," one guy said. "It's just like beer pong." The others laughed as one of the young men took careful aim at the glass bowls.

Ally suddenly approached the guy. "Hey, Zach."

The guy turned around and smiled when he recognized Ally. "Whoa, Ally! Haven't seen you since…my graduation party? Or was it at the beach bonfire last summer?" Zach looked her over and wrapped his arms around her.

Ally closed her eyes and squeezed Zach tighter before she pulled away. Ally didn't take her eyes off his face as she giggled, fumbled with the zipper on her hoodie, and stepped closer to him. "It was the Labor Day beach party at La Jolla Shores. Wow, you look great. You still playing basketball for UCSD?"

Zach handed the ping pong balls to one of his buddies and stepped away from the booth. "Yeah, it's my last year. Then I start law school. Hoping to get into UCLA."

Ally gave Zach a playful punch in the shoulder. "No way! I'll be at UCLA in the fall."

"It's my top school. I'm still waiting to find out if I'll get an interview with the law school admissions team there."

Only a couple feet away, Maddie didn't know if she should join their conversation or stand here by herself. She hadn't heard about a beach bonfire party last summer, nor had she ever heard about this guy. Ally was touchy with Zach, and it was obvious they had some sort of history together.

Ally finally looked back at Maddie and waved for her to come over. "Zach, this is my friend Maddie. She's on the high school surf team. Been their top surfer for a while now."

"Wow, cool. Do you know Drew Richards and Colin Fong?"

"Colin's my cousin, and Drew is a friend of mine. We used to train together."

"Zach got a basketball scholarship to play at UCSD." Ally set her hand on Zach's arm and smiled. "I guess we should get going. Give me a call if you plan to be up in L.A."

They said their goodbyes and continued on their way. Ally kept chatting away, but Maddie didn't say a word. She furrowed her brow and ran her eyes over the wide thoroughfare as they plodded forward, wandering past more carnival games.

Ally stopped walking and reached for Maddie's arm. "I can tell you're upset. I've known you long enough to know when something's bugging you."

"You and Zach seem pretty close." Maddie kept her eyes on a nearby ring toss game.

"Zach and I dated when I was a freshman. We were together for about a year but then broke up right after I started tenth grade. Once he became a senior, he turned into such a jerk."

"He didn't seem like a jerk just now."

"He's matured a lot since he's been in college."

"So, he went to our school when I was there?"

"Yeah, but I doubt you would've remembered him because he ended up graduating early and moving to San Diego." Ally got quiet for a moment and folded her arms as she stared at the ground. "We hooked up last summer…after the beach bonfire. We were both pretty drunk. Not the best experience for my first time."

Maddie gaped at Ally in disbelief. For weeks, all she and Ally did was kiss and cuddle, yet she'd hooked up with this jerk? The queasiness she'd experienced on the Alpine Bobsleds returned. "So, you got back together with him?"

"No, not really. After the bonfire, we chatted on the phone a few times, but I eventually realized he was still a self-centered asshole and stopped calling him."

"Then why would you tell him to call you if you feel that way?"

"I guess it seemed like the right thing to say. I mean, I'd never get back together with him, but I don't see why we can't be friends."

This conversation really couldn't get any worse. She might as well be up front with Ally. "Is that how you see us? Just friends?"

Ally stepped close to Maddie and suddenly looked so sincere. "I love spending time with you. You know that. You're my best friend."

Now it was Maddie's turn to fold her arms and stare at the ground. "So, that's how you see us...nothing more than best friends."

Ally reached over and set her hand on Maddie's arm. "I don't like to think too much about where we stand...with each other. But why do people have to know about us? It's really none of their fucking business what we do in private. You know I want to hang out with you as much as I can before I move away." Although Ally kept her voice low, she sounded irritated.

"Yeah, me, too," Maddie said quietly. Though she wanted to say much more, she kept her thoughts to herself. Pushing the issue would only push Ally away, and they had so little time left together as it was. Maddie decided to ignore her hurt and try to enjoy the rest of the day. "Maybe it's time for more junk food?" Maddie let out a nervous laugh and looked at the food options nearby.

When they left the fun zone and wandered past a booth selling fries and corn dogs, Ally slowed down and studied the menu. "Wanna share some chili curly fries?"

"Sure, why not? Get me a Coke as well." Maddie handed Ally a five and scoped out the area to find a spot to sit.

The cool breeze from the nearby ocean blew through Maddie's hair as she sat on a bench near the fun zone. Ally returned with the curly fries and Coke. She looked so cute in the sun's late afternoon glow. Fit and tan, Ally possessed such a simple beauty that it often took Maddie's breath away. Since she'd been spending so much time with Maddie at the beach, Ally's dark hair had lightened to a beautiful golden auburn.

With a greasy bowl of curly fries on her lap, Maddie slurped her soda and watched the people flooding past them. Since she'd been training even harder than usual lately, she usually avoided fried food, but right now she couldn't get enough of the curly fries drenched in chili, jalapenos, and melted cheese.

Maddie licked the gooey cheese from her fingers. "Mom and Kai would freak if they knew what I was eating today. At least I'm not competing until next month, but I'll run a couple extra miles tomorrow to burn off all these calories from today."

Ally reached over to grab a couple more curly fries. "With your metabolism, I bet you could eat junk food way more often and never gain weight. You've got the kind of body girls our age would love to have."

"We've still got dinner to think about. Maybe a slice of pizza?"

"This might be it for me." Ally wiped the chili sauce from her lips. "I was thinking maybe we could go for a walk on the beach later."

"Sure, might be nice to get some exercise after everything we ate today. A power walk on the beach is a great idea."

Ally brushed her hand against Maddie's and smiled. "I've got something else in mind. I thought we could watch the sunset while snuggled under a blanket and look at the waves under the moon-light."

Ally's words were a surprise. She never wanted to cuddle anywhere but in the privacy of her bedroom.

"Besides you getting these curly fries, that's the best idea I've heard all day." With sunset only a couple hours away, the air had turned chilly. Glad she always kept a blanket and extra beach towels in the car, Maddie was excited about how this day would end.

"I think we should head to the photo exhibit…so you can see your surprise. I have a feeling you're gonna be happy with what you see." Ally's words sounded playful yet mysterious.

Maddie grinned and followed Ally toward the exhibit halls. They wandered through the crowd until they reached the building where the photos were displayed. The photojournalism section was arranged much like an art show in a fine gallery. Each montage was mounted on a black background and displayed on the wall. The room was dimly lit, but each piece had a dedicated light focused on the photos. Proud that Ally had submitted some of her work and that she'd won first place for artistic composition, Maddie was curious to finally see her project.

Maddie recognized Ally's photos right away. Or more precisely, she saw herself in the images. There were at least a dozen prints of her at the beach and in the ocean. As Maddie took a few steps closer to Ally's photojournalism project, she was stunned at what she saw.

Ally had paired each photo with a quote from Samuel Taylor

Coleridge's poem, "The Rime of the Ancient Mariner." No one else appeared in the photos—just Maddie with her surfboard and the ocean in the background. In the top left corner was a photo of her paddling over the glassy water to the surf zone with these lines from the poem:

Alone, alone, all, all alone,
Alone on a wide wide sea!

Maddie smiled when she saw a photo of her riding the curl of a wave. She'd never realized how serious and fierce she looked while surfing. Below the image were three simple but important words from Coleridge's poem:

Water, water, everywhere.

For the past two years, Maddie rarely missed a day in the ocean. As she looked closely at each photo and the accompanying quotes, she realized that the entire piece told a story that only Ally could have done with her talent as a photographer and her fondness for poetry. But the photos conveyed much more than that—something only the two of them shared.

Under a photo of Maddie standing with her surfboard on the beach in front of the bright red and orange sunset was this line from the poem:

Her *lips were red,* her *looks were free.*

In this image, the ocean reflected the fiery sky. Stunned that Ally had compiled these photos and lines from Coleridge's poem, Maddie didn't know what to say. Taken over the past year, these photos showed the progression of Maddie's ability as a surfer—from a competent beginner to the top competitor on the high school surf team. Every image shone with Ally's understanding of just how important the ocean was to Maddie.

There was a photo of Maddie lying on the sand and dozing, the image taken after she'd spent the day training in Huntington Beach. She laughed when she read the accompanying quote:

Oh sleep! it is a gentle thing.

The next photo was a sensual shot of Maddie in her bikini on the beach at dusk. Ally had focused the image on Maddie's body and blurred the ocean in the background. The surfboard Kai had shaped for her was wedged in the sand next to her. In the photograph, Maddie seemed to be looking way beyond the surf zone. Lavender rays from the setting sun reflected off her face. Maddie had no recollection of Ally taking this photo. Below the photo was a line from Coleridge's poem that made Maddie gasp:

A spring of love gushed from my heart.

Was this quote supposed to describe her love for the ocean or Ally's love for her? Maddie glanced at Ally who'd wandered over to another wall of photos. When their eyes met, Ally smiled then averted her gaze.

Maddie couldn't stop smiling as she again looked at the mosaic of photos and quotes. The most striking photo of all was placed in the center—an image of Maddie exiting the curl of a huge wave with these words below it:

The fair breeze blew, the white foam flew,
The furrow followed free:
We were the first that ever burst
Into that silent sea.

Right now, this was enough for Maddie. It had to be. No need for embraces or hands clasped with others around. No need for public declarations of love. Sometimes no spoken words were needed to convey how someone felt about another person. These quotes and photos were enough.

Chapter Eleven

Huntington Beach, California: August 2000

Adrenalin and nerves coursed through Maddie's body, making her jittery and sick to her stomach. She studied the waves, paced along the sand, and waited for her group to be called. The other three girls competing in her group stood a few feet away with their boards waxed and ready. They looked way more muscular and fit compared to her, more confident and tough.

Over the past few years, Maddie had gone from a competent surfer to a champ. Now, at only eighteen years old, she'd qualified for the U.S. Open of Surfing. In fifteen minutes, she'd be called to the line-up, and in another fifteen she'd be in the water. In a long-sleeved Quiksilver rash guard, she felt overheated under the mid-day sun. Next to her, Kai kept a close eye on the ocean while he assessed how the waves were breaking.

Behind Maddie stood her mom and Ally. Although home on summer break, Ally had barely been able to hang out. Her family had apparently wanted her with them as much as possible. It was bad enough that they barely spoke on the phone anymore since Ally's college schedule was so full. She'd also been aloof lately and less affectionate. Ally had dropped by Royal Palace a few times, but always before Maddie arrived and never stayed long once she did. But she'd also made the time to watch Maddie compete. That meant a lot.

The sand was covered with spectators and film crews. Some of the former members of the high school surf team stood nearby to support Maddie, including Colin and Drew. Over the past few months, Maddie and Drew had become close friends. Though he'd asked a couple months ago if he could be her date to her prom, she turned him down. There was only one person she wanted to go with.

The swell had dropped a bit, and the waves were weak and mushy. Though Maddie could handle larger waves, smaller waves were more of a challenge since she had to work harder to dip into the curl and catch the momentum. This was much different than surfing in San Clemente or at Black's Beach. This was the U.S.

Open where, if she won third place or higher in her age group, she could go on to compete all over the world.

Way behind the film crews and spectators, ambulances filled the first few slots in the parking lot. For big surf competitions, they had medics on hand, but most of the medical issues at these events were minor—abrasions, contusions, heat exhaustion, dehydration.

Maddie stepped closer to Kai and peered past the surf line to see if the swell was building. "Seems like the waves are getting smaller."

"Nah, it's just a bad set." Kai used his binoculars to get a better view of the surf. "The sets have been steady all morning, and the breaks are clean. You've mastered all different types of waves. There's nothing you can't handle, even small and mushy waves like these."

Maddie barely heard what Kai said. "What if I'm not as good as my competitors? I might not even make it past the first heat. That one girl from Australia was the second-ranked junior world champ from last summer. She hasn't lost any competitions all year."

Kai lowered his binoculars and waved an arm toward Maddie's competitors. "*Keiki*, you wouldn't be here if you weren't as good as them. You got this."

The waves surged toward shore. Maddie's breathing refused to calm. With ten minutes to go until she'd be called to the line-up, she was nauseous. Sweat dripped down her face. "What if, during my heat, there's a really long lull between sets? Or what if the waves during my heat suck? They only give us twenty minutes in the water."

Kai placed a beaded bracelet in her palm and cupped his hand over hers. "Remember what I told you about turning off the negative thoughts. You take it one wave at a time, one heat at a time, one victory at a time. Not just anyone can compete in the U.S. Open. Only the best ones qualify. It's your turn to wear this bracelet. You've more than proven yourself as one of the top surfers in Southern California."

This was Kai's bracelet. He'd worn it for as long as Maddie could remember. She ran her fingers over the koa wood and slipped it around her wrist. Kai tightened the leather string snug, and Maddie smiled—proud to now be the one to wear this.

"Wow, thanks." Maddie gave Kai a quick hug. As she admired the polished beads, she took a couple of slow and deep breaths and felt a bit calmer. In a few minutes, she would charge toward the waves and do her best to impress the judges.

Kai looped the leash around Maddie's ankle and draped his arm around her shoulder. Mom, Colin, Drew, and Ally stood nearby as they all clapped and called out her name.

"*Aloha wau iā 'oe*," Kai said quietly and kissed Maddie on the cheek.

"Love you, too." Maddie leaned into Kai as she took a few more slow and steady breaths.

"You got this, cousin." Colin slapped a hand on her back.

"Go out there and have fun," Drew said, then gave her a side-ways hug.

Her mother set her hand on Maddie's cheek. "Honey, I'm so proud of you, no matter if you come in first, second, or last."

Happy that Mom had taken the day off to be here, Maddie hugged her and was grateful she'd given up so much to get her to this point in her young surfing career.

Ally lightly touched Maddie's arm with her fingertips. She stepped close and whispered in her ear, "You're the best surfer here today. I just know it. I'll be on shore cheering you on."

The soft breath on her skin sent a chill down Maddie's spine, and the last of the nervousness melted away. She was ready to ride the waves.

A horn blared from behind her, and the speakers crackled. "Group five, head to the line-up! One minute until your heat begins."

Maddie gripped her board and took her position at the starting point on the damp sand. Her legs were tense and ready to leap into action. A fire coursed through her body.

The horn sounded, and Maddie and the other three women sprinted into the water. Maddie hopped on her board and sliced her hands through the water, making it to the surf zone first. After she dove under a small wave, she got in position and lay atop her board as she waited. Only small tumblers churned toward shore, nothing big enough or rideable so far, but one of her competitors managed to get up on a small breaker, displaying only mediocre techniques to the judges.

Five minutes passed, and Maddie hadn't even caught a small

wave. She knew she could do better than this girl. Maddie only had a mere fifteen minutes to show the judges she was the best. Then, out in the distance, she saw it: the lip of a wave beginning to break. She paddled with all her might to get to the base of the wave, and within seconds she was up on her board and riding the curl. She was in top form, confident and stylish in her techniques, even going aerial at the end of her ride. The board hit the water with a loud smack, and she effortlessly rode out the rest of the wave.

Maddie paddled back to the line-up and quickly dropped into another wave. When she zipped down the face, she heard the spectators cheering on shore and the commentator telling the crowd through the loudspeaker about her techniques. At the end of her ride, she shot through the barrel and popped out the other side.

Back she went to the surf zone. She likely only had ten more minutes to impress the judges with a couple more rides, but there was a lull in between sets. The ocean was flat as a lake with no breakers in sight. Maddie took a moment to catch her breath and take in what was happening on shore. The judges were still sitting behind tables under the blue canopies, waiting for the competitors to catch a wave. Mom was standing next to Kai, and Colin and Ally were sitting close together on the sand. Maddie returned her attention to the competition. Still nothing formed in the water, but Maddie waited patiently. She only needed one more impressive ride to gain more points in this heat.

A quick glance back at shore revealed the judges still had their binoculars poised and ready, never taking their eyes off the surfers. Maddie again noticed Ally sitting next to Colin, but this time they sat even closer together. Though she couldn't be sure from this distance, it looked like Ally's arm was draped over Colin's leg and his hand was in hers.

A movement from the corner of her eye caught her attention. The waves were starting to pick up. Maddie got back into position and waited, but she couldn't resist a final quick glance at the shore. This time, she saw something unexpected: Colin leaning over to kiss Ally. Maddie had to squint to make sure she'd seen things correctly. This time she saw it clearly—the two of them making out.

Why would Ally be kissing Colin?

Maddie's eyes welled up with tears. Her chest tightened, and it was hard to breathe. A wave approached, the biggest one so far in this heat. At the base of the face, she automatically sliced her hands through the water, barely registering its flow. The power of the wave caught the momentum of her board, but she was so unfocused and distracted that she dropped out of it. Maddie paddled to get back in the line-up, but her attention was behind her, on the shore. Ally and Colin were still sitting close together and still making out.

Why would Colin be kissing Ally, the girl she loved? For the past year, Ally seemed as uninterested in guys as Maddie was. She'd never mentioned a boyfriend. And when had she even had time for Colin, when she'd barely had time for Maddie? But then it hit her. Ally would go to Royal Palace when Colin was there and chat with him before Maddie showed up. And when Maddie did show up, Ally would leave.

How could Maddie have not noticed this? Ally had a boyfriend—and it was Maddie's own cousin.

Another wave was coming her way. Maddie had a few seconds to make a decision: keep on surfing or keep staring at the shore? She chose to focus on the competition and do her best to win. With a deep breath, she got into position to enter the barrel. She was just about in the tube but couldn't quite pick up enough speed to stay ahead of the whitewash at the front of the wave. This was the last chance to earn more points in this heat, so Maddie took the risk and stood up anyway. It was the wrong move. She lost her balance and went over the falls—her board and body churning in the wave. Stuck in the whitewater, Maddie struggled to reach the surface and catch her breath. Another breaking wave surged over her.

Caught inside, Maddie's body tumbled out of control in the surf. Her surfboard spun around in the wave and sailed right at her. Unable to duck in time, the surfboard whacked her in the face, and the fin sliced her cheek. The jostling of the breaker flipped her head back and then whipped her neck from side to side. She felt a pop in her neck—the pain instant and intense. When the force of another wave pushed her to the floor of the ocean, Maddie couldn't tell which way was up or down.

The next thing she knew, hands gripped her arms, and she was helped to the surface. She gasped for air. Another breaker approached. Maddie opened her eyes enough to see the red trunks of a lifeguard as he guided her under the wave. When they emerged on the other side, the lifeguard looped a rescue tube around her waist.

"I got you," he said. His tone was firm and reassuring. The lifeguard slipped his arm under Maddie's armpit and across her chest as he kept her head above water and kicked hard to get her out of the surf zone.

Different than that horrible night in Clear Springs Lake when Maddie tried to help Brooke to shore, the lifeguard effortlessly kept Maddie afloat until they were in the shallow area. Another guard tromped through the water and lifted Maddie into his arms and carried her to the beach.

As she lay on the warm sand, she raised a hand to her face and felt warm blood pouring from a huge gash in her cheek—the blood dripping down her neck and onto her rash guard. How could she have wiped out on a four-foot wave? They'd likely pull her from the competition for this stupid cut on her face.

Maddie tried to find Mom and Kai, but she could only hear their voices. Trying hard to focus, she blinked a few times, but everything was blurry. Not able to see their expressions or make out what they were saying, Maddie knew her mom was probably a wreck right now at the sight of all this blood. Maddie heard the panic in her mom's voice. One lifeguard held a gauze pad on Maddie's cheek; another one packed sand around her head and neck. This must be a precaution for any surfer who went over the falls, so she waited while the guards assessed her condition.

Since she had feeling in her hands and feet, her fall had to have been minor. She'd had worse tumbles in much rougher surf. Pissed that this wipe-out would likely prevent her from competing in the next round, Maddie let the guards tend to her facial laceration. She felt well enough to hit the surf again, but she knew what the lifeguards and judges would say. In a matter of seconds, her chances of competing all over the world were probably over—at least for this season.

Maddie heard Kai talking to the lifeguards, and then she overheard her mom speaking to them. She heard Drew asking Kai a bunch of questions. His voice sounded overly concerned and frantic, but because too many people were speaking at the same time, Maddie couldn't make out what any of them were saying. All she wanted to do was get up from the sand, admit defeat, and go home. She saw that a big crowd had formed around her, along with what looked to be two paramedics. Ally and Colin were nowhere to be found.

Angela kneeled at Maddie's side. "Sweetie, they think it's best to transport you to the hospital."

"The hospital? Mom, I'm fine. It's just a bad cut from the fin." Maddie's cheek stung from the laceration, but the ache in her neck grew more intense, with the pain now radiating into her head.

Angela held Maddie's hand. "Honey, the cut's really deep."

Maddie tried to reach up to touch the laceration, but Angela held her hand away from her face. "How bad is it? Why can't you just drive me to urgent care?"

"This is likely gonna take more than a few stitches. The medic said you might need surgery, just based on the size of the cut."

"Surgery?" Maddie's voice broke, and tears flooded from her eyes.

Angela leaned closer to Maddie. "Sweetie, they'll get you all fixed up at the hospital. A plastic surgeon will likely make sure there's hardly any scarring."

"Hardly any scarring? How big is the cut?" Maddie started sobbing. Would she now be ugly and disfigured?

Kai crouched down next to Maddie and Angela. "*Keiki*, the fin got you real bad. Can't hurt to have them do a thorough exam at the hospital. Won't be surprised if you got whiplash. It looked like the board whacked your head pretty hard. You might even have a concussion."

When the paramedics and lifeguards scooted a backboard under her body, Maddie sobbed harder. Someone placed some sort of tape across her forehead, stabilizing her head on the backboard. She had no say in whether she could just go home or have her mom take her to urgent care to get the cut on her face stitched up. But she might be more injured than she originally thought. The pain had become so bad that she thought she was going to throw up.

"Angie, you ride along in the ambulance," Kai said. "I'll follow in the truck. Drew said he'll pack up all our gear and call his dad. He said he's on call this weekend."

"Is the hospital in Huntington the best one around here for head injuries?" Angela said quietly, her voice quivering. "As well as spinal injuries?"

Maddie couldn't stop shivering. "They think I have a spinal cord injury? And a head injury?" Maddie's fears intensified by the second. But she had complete sensation in her arms and feet. People who break their necks can't feel anything in their extremities. She couldn't have broken her neck. Or did she?

"Honey, they'll get you to the hospital soon. I'll stay with you for as long as they let me." Angela released Maddie's hand and stood to the side.

Maddie wiggled her toes and fingers—her own little test to see how hurt she was. With full movement in her arms and feet, she could walk off the sand and to the parking lot right now if they let her.

When the lifeguards carried Maddie atop the backboard across the sand and to the idling ambulance, the horn blasted for the next heat to begin. This should've been her second heat, the one that might've earned her the most points, but victory had slipped away in a matter of seconds with that stupid wipe-out.

Determined to not stay out of the water for too long, Maddie decided right then and there that she'd be surfing again in a couple days. Or next week at the latest. She was sure that a ride in an ambulance to the ER was a waste of time; they'd get her to the hospital and determine she was totally fine except for the gash in her cheek. But once they lifted her body onto a stretcher and scooted her into the ambulance, the pain in her neck got even worse. So maybe she was wrong. Maybe she might not be back in the water next week after all.

Chapter Twelve

Maddie awoke to see Kai and Mom standing on each side of the bed. Not able to turn her head to look at their expressions, Maddie struggled to keep her eyes open. The morphine kept her groggy, and the rigid brace around her neck prevented her from doing much besides raise an arm or move her eyes to see which nurse entered the room to give her more pain meds or check her vitals. Even though she wanted to read the novel her mom brought to the hospital, Maddie was too fuzzy-headed to concentrate, so for now she kept the book on the little table next to the bed.

Although sleepy, Maddie managed to open her eyes enough to see the worried looks on Kai's and Mom's faces. The late afternoon sun shone through the window, causing Maddie to squint at the glaring light. Despite being on morphine since yesterday when she got to the ER, she still experienced some pain, but the medication kept her foggy enough to not really care how bad the pain was. A thick bandage covered her left cheek. Although the fracture in one of the vertebrae in her neck was tiny, the brace would be necessary for a while to keep her neck stabilized.

"How ya doin', *keiki*?" Kai leaned over and cupped his hand over Maddie's. "You need more pain meds? How about some ice water or apple juice?"

"Maybe later," Maddie said, her voice hoarse.

Kai hadn't left Maddie's side since they moved her to a room last night. She vaguely recalled Mom urging Kai to go home when she left around midnight, but he refused, saying he'd sleep in the chair. Dark circles had formed under his eyes, and he was still in his sweatshirt and board shorts from yesterday. Maddie noticed how grey Kai's hair had become this past year. Right now, he looked more like a man in his sixties than forties.

Kai squeezed Maddie's hand. "You're a tough one. You had me scared when they first got you out of the water, but then I realized this is our brave Maddie. Like I always say, there's not much you can't handle in the ocean. You were in top form yesterday, but then it's like something changed when you were on that wave."

     Caught Inside

"Guess I can't handle four-foot waves." Maddie averted her gaze from Kai's and winced as the cut on her face started to throb.

"You were doing fine up until then. You get a cramp in your leg or something? Or were you scared? I haven't seen you afraid of the waves since I took you out during that huge south swell from the big hurricane last summer. Did *maka'u* get in the way?"

"Kai, let her rest. She's been through a lot." Angela smoothed out the covers and set her hand on Maddie's arm. "Honey, you might be due for more pain meds. It's best you get some rest and not think much about what happened yesterday."

"Mom, it's okay. I don't mind talking about it. Might as well try to learn from my mistakes. Kai, you know I'm not afraid of the waves, no matter how big they are."

Kai leaned back in the chair and ran a hand through his messy hair. "Drew says the judges gave you high scores for the waves you caught. You were in the lead until you fell. But, no worries. Even the best surfers wipe out from time to time. This was only one competition out of many more to come."

"Long after she heals." Angela ran her fingers through Maddie's hair. "And no surf competitions if the waves are really big."

Maddie blinked up at the ceiling, not sure what she should tell Kai about yesterday. Now that she felt a little less loopy, the memories returned. She could've won the heat had she not been preoccupied with what she'd seen. Kai was right; there wasn't much she couldn't handle in the water. It was what happened on shore that she couldn't handle.

"I guess I got distracted and lost focus," Maddie finally said.

"Distracted? From what? Was it the girl who was shredding it on the waves? Sure, she was good, but you're just as good on the board. Remember, during competitions you hafta surf like nobody's around."

"It wasn't *that* girl who distracted me." After she glanced at her mom, who'd walked over to the window to lower the blinds, Maddie gave Kai a pleading look, hoping he'd figure out what she was trying to say.

Kai nodded, his eyes widening. "Yeah, a lot was happening yesterday."

Kai was the only one who knew Maddie had a crush on Ally, despite not having said much more than she enjoyed being around her and liked lots of things about her. However, Maddie never told Kai she longed to have Ally as her girlfriend—someone to take to dinner and to the movies like a normal couple would do. She had certainly never revealed to anyone that she and Ally would sometimes make out in the privacy of their bedrooms. Although California was a whole lot different than Mississippi as far as being more liberal, a guy liking another guy or a girl liking another girl wasn't totally accepted.

"You know, *keiki*, I learned long ago that some things are out of our control, like the way a wave breaks or how an unexpected wind swell changes the shape of a wave. You can't control the size or shape of a wave, but you can control how you handle it."

The truth of Kai's words hit her almost as hard as her surfboard. Ally would never love her. And there was nothing Maddie could do to change that.

She closed her eyes and swallowed, hoping tears wouldn't fall. It had been ridiculous to think that Ally would ever be in a full-on relationship with her. She'd even messed up an important surf competition because of a girl! The kisses they'd once shared had not meant as much to Ally as they did to Maddie. In Ally's world, girls dated boys, and boys kissed girls. Maybe it'd be better if Maddie was part of that world, too.

Maddie stared at the ceiling and wondered what Ally was doing right now, but she quickly put that thought out of her mind. After what happened yesterday, she didn't want to see Ally or talk to her. Maddie hid her heartbreak and smiled at Kai. "After yesterday, I know I won't ever let anything distract me when I'm surfing."

"Sometimes it takes something bad happening to make you realize what's important to you. Or who's important to you."

"Or who isn't important," Maddie said quietly and reached for Kai's hand.

Kai leaned closer to Maddie's ear and whispered, "Sometimes we don't end up with our first love, but that person will always remind us of how we learned to open our heart to love. I'm just glad you weren't hurt more than you were yesterday." Kai's eyes were filled with tears. He looked like he had more to say, but he remained quiet and squeezed her hand.

In all the time Maddie had known Kai, he'd been upbeat and positive. Never teary like this. Maddie squeezed his hand back. "There will always be more competitions. Next time I won't get distracted."

Kai looked at Angela and then at Maddie. "Maddie, I wanna tell you something I've been wanting to say for a real long time. When I met your mom, I knew I couldn't let her go. Right away, I knew she was the one."

"Honey, I'm sure Maddie doesn't want to hear anything sappy right now." Angela walked up to him and kissed him on the cheek. "Just let her rest."

"I'll be real quick. See, after I met your mom, I never expected I'd get to hang out with such a cool kid and teach her how to surf. I never had a child of my own, but you've been such an amazing gift to me. When you got hurt yesterday, my heart broke for you. I realize it's because I see you like my own child, my *hānai* daughter."

With tears in her eyes, Angela stood behind Kai and put her arm around his shoulders. Before Maddie had a chance to ask Kai what *hānai* meant, he explained.

"In Hawaii, people sometimes welcome someone into their life just like their own daughter or son. It's an ancient Hawaiian tradition, but in more simple terms, to *hānai* means to informally adopt someone. I'll always love you like my own child."

Not able to articulate what she really wanted to say, about how she saw Kai as a father, Maddie simply said, "*Aloha wau iā 'oe*" and reached for his hand.

Kai used his sleeve to wipe away his tears. "Remember that Hawaiian song I sometimes sing as we're heading out to the waves?"

"How could I forget? You sing it just about every time we hit the surf. I'm surprised you haven't made me learn the song on the ukulele." Maddie laughed, hopeful that her comment would lighten the situation.

"Toward the end of the song, the words don't just describe surfing. The lyrics say something about how the timid bird has retired to the mountaintop and that the path ahead is precarious— just like a swaying tightrope. *Keiki*, if you ever feel like you're gonna fall from that tightrope, just know I'll always be there to catch you."

Maddie started to cry. Tears of joy. Tears of gratitude. But also tears of uncertainty about whether she'd be healed enough to ever be a top-ranked surfer. As tears flowed from her eyes, she couldn't say everything that was in her heart. More than her surfing coach and Mom's boyfriend, Kai filled a huge hole in Maddie's life that she didn't know was there until now.

Kai and Angela leaned over the bed and attempted to hug Maddie, but when she gasped in pain, they stepped back. Embarrassed about crying, she laughed and said, "You two probably need more Kleenex than I do."

Her comment made Angela cry even more and caused Kai to chuckle, but for Maddie it put a stop to her silly tears. For once in her life, she finally had a complete family unit. Though not her legal or biological father, Kai made Maddie feel like he'd take care of her and would always be there. He'd be there for big life events—graduations, other surfing competitions, maybe even her wedding one day.

"Knock-knock," Maddie heard a man say as he entered the room.

Although she couldn't see him, Maddie recognized Doctor Richards's voice. She'd grown tired of hearing the doctors and nurses announce their entrance into the room with that annoying "knock-knock" announcement.

"Hey, Jerry." Kai stood to greet Doctor Richards and shook his hand. "Thanks for taking care of our girl."

When Doctor Richards stood by Maddie's side, he raised the bed and adjusted the pillows behind her head. "You're doing well, considering the extent of your injuries. You've been good about asking for pain medication when you need it, right?"

Maddie tried to nod, but the stiff neck brace prevented her from being able to move anything above her chest. "The pain's getting pretty bad again, especially from the gash on my face. The neck pain hasn't let up at all. My headache's coming back, too."

"The headache is pretty normal, even for a minor concussion. We need to get your pain level to a much more manageable level. As soon as I finish examining you, I'll have the nurse come in and give you more meds."

Maddie lifted a hand and touched the thick bandage covering her cheek. "I can't believe I had to have surgery to fix a cut from a surf fin."

"In all the years I've been surfing, I've actually seen much worse. I talked to the plastic surgeon this morning. She assured me that the scar on your face will fade over time. The only evidence of the laceration will be a thin white line. You'll have quite a story to tell your kids someday. The cut is pretty minor compared to the neck injury."

"You think she'll be able to surf like she did before?" Kai asked.

"We're going to have to take it one week at a time. Maddie's young and fit, but the next two weeks will be crucial as far as determining how well she heals. Maddie, let's have you grip my fingers." Doctor Richards held out his hands. "I was pleased to find out the CT scan showed there's no brain bleed, but the neurologist told me he'd like to do a repeat scan later tonight and again tomorrow to make sure things are stable."

Maddie squeezed the doctor's fingers. Annoyed with the frequent exams by the doctors and the repeated questions about what year it was or who the president was, she tried her best to be nice to Doctor Richards since he was Drew's dad. It was fortunate he'd been on call when she was taken to the hospital because he was able to expedite the tests and procedures.

Doctor Richards released his fingers from Maddie's grip. "I'd imagine you'll go home in a week or so. The more we can keep your neck immobilized while you're in the hospital, the better. Once home, you'll be on total bed rest for a while, but I think you'll be totally healed and back in the water by early spring."

"By spring?" Maddie said, her tone escalating. "That's half a year away! I can't stay out of the water that long. I need to stay in top shape for the next competition."

Angela gripped Maddie's hand. "Honey, the competitions can wait. You're lucky you're not paralyzed."

"Mom, six months is a long time to not surf!"

Kai crossed his arms and paced to the window. "*Keiki*, you'll be as good as ever once you're fully recovered."

Maddie frowned and tried to fight off the tears that brimmed at her eyes. "You all don't get it. I can't even handle having to stay out of the water for more than a week."

Doctor Richards pulled a chair close to the side of the bed and sat down. "Kiddo, trust me, I get it. When I was sixteen, I broke my leg skateboarding. The doctor said I couldn't surf for eight weeks. That just about killed me to not be able to surf for that long."

"Eight weeks is a lot different than six months." Maddie's

voice broke, and the tears now flowed freely.

Doctor Richards handed Maddie a tissue and set his hand on her arm. "You need to understand how serious your injury is. The concussion is minor compared to the broken neck. Although the fracture to the C-6 vertebra is small, what we'd consider a hairline fracture, you still sustained a serious neck injury. You'll be in the cervical brace for six to eight weeks. In a few weeks we'll have you start physical therapy for a couple months to strengthen your muscles and expedite your recovery."

"Two months of PT? Can I at least swim during that time?"

Doctor Richards stood and leaned in closer to examine the stiff brace around Maddie's neck. "You'll have to stay out of the water for several weeks. That means not even a quick dip in the ocean on a calm day. We'll leave it up to your physical therapist to decide when you're ready to swim. You have to understand this isn't just a simple case of whiplash. If you start surfing when you're not fully healed, it'll likely lead to a significant setback and further damage."

Kai took the seat that Doctor Richards vacated. "I'll set you up with a bunch of surfing movies to keep you busy while you're recovering."

"That'll just make me miss it even more." Maddie dabbed her eyes with the tissue.

"Not unless you use those videos to study how the surfers handle huge waves in places like Australia and Hawaii. I've got a copy of a great documentary called *Beyond Blazing Boards*. They show some of the best surfers ripping down the faces of the tallest waves you'll ever see on film. These big wave riders are probably—"

"Honey, she's not going to surf big waves ever again." Angela gave Kai a stern look, which quickly shut him up.

After Doctor Richards said goodbye and left, Maddie heard someone else enter the room, but she couldn't see who it was since the cervical brace again prevented her from turning her head. Nurses and doctors came in and out of her room so frequently that Maddie expected it to be another person checking her vitals or giving her more meds. The person came into sight. It was Drew. Tired of people coming and going as they pleased, Maddie hoped he wouldn't stay long because she just wanted to sleep.

Angela smiled when Drew got closer. "Hi, Drew. So nice of

you to visit Maddie. Your dad has been a godsend while Maddie recovers from the accident."

Drew stepped into Maddie's line of sight so she didn't have to move her head. He had a wrapped gift wedged under his arm. "My dad said it was okay for me to come in to see you now. I've been waiting in the hallway until he finished talking to you. Colin and Ally are down in the lobby. They pulled into the parking lot right when I did."

Her body tensed. "Figures they'd drive here together," Maddie muttered. She took a couple deep breaths as she fought back the tears. When Kai reached over to set a hand on her arm, she felt a bit calmer.

"I got this for you." Drew handed Maddie a gift: something rectangular, solid, and wrapped in pink paper. He stuffed his hands in his pockets.

Angela raised the bed higher so Maddie could more easily see Drew. After Angela tucked the covers around Maddie's body, she grabbed her purse and kissed Maddie on the forehead. "You get some rest. Kai and I are going to get something to eat."

"Mom, if you see Colin and Ally in the lobby, can you tell them I'm not up for any more visitors? If they're not there, call Colin to say I'm too tired to see them."

"All right, sweetie." Angela slipped her hand in Kai's. It took her a moment to pull Kai away from Maddie's side, but the two of them said their goodbyes and left Drew alone with Maddie.

But just as soon as Mom and Kai left, the nurse came in to do a blood pressure check and to give Maddie another dose of morphine directly through the IV. Maddie gave the nurse a thumbs up, who wrote something on the whiteboard mounted on the wall, returned the thumbs up, and left.

"So, um, do you want me to help you open it?" Drew gestured to the wrapped gift.

"I can do it." Maddie tore off the pink tissue paper to find a book titled *The Sea, the Sea* by Iris Murdoch. Her sadness and annoyance were replaced with excitement as she skimmed the details on the back cover. She could dive into this novel as soon as she finished the one she was currently reading. Maybe recovering from her accident wouldn't be as boring as she thought.

"I picked that one because of the waves on the cover." Drew laughed. "The sticker on the front of the book says it won a

Booker Prize. I'm not sure what that is, but I figured it must be a good book if it won a prize and has waves on the cover. Plus, I know how you like British authors."

How had Drew known her preference in reading material? She'd never told him how much she enjoyed reading novels by British authors. The morphine started to kick in, making her a bit woozy.

"*The Voyage Out*," Drew read from the cover of the book on the side table. "You reading ahead for one of your English classes at Chapman?"

"No, just reading it for fun, but the pain meds make it hard for me to focus on the words." Although Maddie had only read five of Virginia Woolf's books, *The Voyage Out* intrigued her almost as much as *To the Lighthouse*. "I'm excited to learn more about Woolf and other authors when I start college in the fall. I was stoked to find out I got a merit scholarship to help make Chapman a reality."

Drew opened the book at the bookmark and carefully studied the page. "This book seems pretty interesting, something about going down some river in London. Like here it says, 'They were now moving steadily down the river, passing the dark shapes of ships at anchor, and London was a swarm of lights with a pale-yellow canopy drooping above it.'"

Mesmerized by Drew's cadence, she hoped he'd continue reading, but he didn't. "Virginia Woolf writes a lot about London," Maddie said. "She's describing the Thames, the long river that runs through the city."

Drew returned the book to the side table. "That passage kinda reminds me of a book I read by Charles Dickens, except his description of London is much bleaker than this. All I remember reading in *Great Expectations* is that it was a dangerous and dirty city. Woolf makes it sound like a nice place, especially this river."

"One day I'd like to go to London. Lots of famous authors lived there. Seems like such an interesting place to visit, especially since I'm majoring in English. I'd like to study in England, but my mom probably wouldn't like me being away for such a long time."

"If that's what you wanna do, you should do it. I mean, I know our parents probably have their own idea of what they want us to do, but if you wanna go to school in England, then you should do it. My dad keeps pushing me to become a doctor, but that's not what I want to do. I wanna teach music and be a musician. Not like in a rock band or anything. I mean a musician in a professional symphony."

"Does your dad know you don't want to be a doctor?"

"We've never talked about it. He hears me practice my cello all the time, even says how good I am, but I think he sees this as some sort of hobby and not anything that'd ever make me rich or successful. My dad's so used to us both excelling at the same things."

"Like surfing?" Maddie paid close attention to the way Drew lit up when she asked that question. She loved how he was as into surfing as she was but also had other more intellectual interests, just like she did.

"Yeah, especially surfing. Don't get me wrong. I love to surf, but that's probably the only good thing my dad and I have in common."

Maddie waited for Drew to say more, but after a few silent moments she said, "You should do what you want to do. Maybe your dad will see how good you are and realize you should follow your dream of being a musician."

"Yeah, hopefully." Drew stuffed his hands in his pockets and leaned against the bed. He suddenly seemed nervous. He cleared his throat and glanced again at the Woolf novel sitting on the table. Keeping his eyes on the book, he stammered, "So, I know you said you weren't…well, interested in dating me, but I was thinking…maybe we can just hang out. I mean, maybe do more stuff together as friends. Maybe we could go to the movies and get dinner sometimes."

"Your dad says I'll be on total bed rest for a while. I won't be able to do much besides watch TV and read, but maybe we can hang out at my house while I recover. You could bring over some DVDs for us to watch."

"That'd be cool." Drew grinned, the smile lighting up his entire face.

Though Maddie had only ever considered Drew a surfing buddy, maybe she needed to be like a typical teenage girl who dated guys. Or at least give it a try. He was good-looking, for a guy, but right now she was mostly captivated by his intense blue eyes and cute smile. "Once I'm healed up, it'd be nice to go out. I mean, on a real date." As soon as the words left her mouth, Maddie's heart pounded hard. Her misgivings about dating Drew were making themselves known, but she ignored them.

"Really? That'd be great." Drew kept smiling, and then he picked up the Woolf book from the table. "If you want, I can read this to you. I mean, just to help you pass the time while you're stuck in the hospital."

"I'd like that. You're sure you don't mind?" Maddie reached over to set her hand atop Drew's for a few seconds before she moved it back to her lap. Touched that Drew would take the time to read to her, Maddie was glad he'd come to visit. Drew had gone to all of her surf competitions and was one of the nicest guys she knew. He'd been there for her no matter what and would probably be a sweet boyfriend. Though she knew she liked girls, Maddie figured she should at least give Drew a chance.

"It's not like I have to get home right away. My dad knows where I am." Drew dragged the chair closer to the side of the bed and began to read from the page where he left off earlier. "'There were the lights of the great theatres…the lights of the long streets, lights that indicated huge squares of domestic comfort, lights that hung high in air. No darkness would ever settle upon those lamps, as no darkness had settled upon them for hundreds of years.'"

Drew read at a steady pace, and his warm voice brought the book to life. He spoke at just the right volume, paused in the right places, and emphasized certain words when necessary. Maddie closed her eyes and became even more drowsy. She imagined one day traveling to the United Kingdom—to experience the sights and sounds that Virginia Woolf wrote about in her novels. Maybe she'd go alone; maybe she'd go with Drew or someone else altogether. Not Ally, though. That chapter of Maddie's life was over. It was time for something new.

Chapter Thirteen

San Onofre, California: December 2000

With only a couple hours until sunset, the sun barely peeked through the dark clouds over the ocean. The tumblers came in fast with hardly any breaks in between sets. A heavy wind from the north churned up the water, creating lots of whitewash. It'd been a while since Maddie had seen whitecaps like these. The air temp hadn't gone above sixty all week, and it had been cloudy for the past few days. Usually a busy beach during spring and summer, San Onofre State Beach was nearly vacant this afternoon except for a few surfers out in the water and a couple walkers on shore. Maddie gazed at the rough surf, zipped up her hoodie, and put her hands in the pockets. Even in a long-sleeved T-shirt and a thick hoodie and sweats, she shivered from the cold air.

When Drew pulled into the dirt parking lot, Maddie waved to let him know she'd secured a spot by a fire pit. While he parked and hauled a stack of logs to the beach, Maddie went to her SUV to get the food she'd picked up from Royal Palace. With only one more week until winter break, Maddie and Drew hardly had time for dates, so they had to squeeze in moments together between classes and work. A sick feeling traveled from her throat to the pit of her stomach as she thought about this afternoon's date with Drew.

Drew tossed a thick blanket on the sand and wrapped his arms around Maddie. "This fleece blanket should keep us warm later tonight. I also brought a tent. I figured it might get cold once the sun goes down."

"You always think of everything." Maddie let out a quiet, nervous laugh. Her stomach did flip-flops. Though Drew held her close, she still shivered from the cold air.

"Maybe I should start the fire now and get you warmed up."

"No, let's wait. I think after I have some of Mom's soup, I'll be fine."

Maddie buried her face in Drew's chest. She'd already rehearsed this conversation in her head several times on her drive to the beach this afternoon. As Drew held her tighter, he kissed the top of her head and slid his hands down her back. Always so gentle, Drew's touch made her feel safe and calm.

Maddie pulled back from Drew's embrace and bit her lower lip. "I'm not sure if this is the best day for this," she said quietly without looking at him. "I know how excited you were about today being the day I finally—"

"Babe, you don't have to do this if you don't feel ready." Drew slipped his hand in Maddie's. "I mean, it's not like today has to be the day for this to happen."

As Maddie studied the breakers headed toward shore, she leaned against Drew and set her head on his shoulder. "I thought for sure I'd be ready to do this today, but now I'm having second thoughts."

"You'll know when you're ready." Drew kissed Maddie on the forehead and pulled her closer.

"I know my physical therapist said it's okay for me to get back in the water, but I'm not even sure I can paddle out past these shore breakers. The waves look pretty rough." Though she finished physical therapy last month, Maddie still experienced weakness in her back and shoulders and didn't think she had the strength or stamina to reach the surf zone.

While Drew gazed at the ocean, he stood behind Maddie and wrapped his arms around her. "Past these shore breakers, the waves actually look pretty mushy."

Maddie stepped away from the warmth of Drew's arms and watched the waves crash on shore. She tensed, recalling how she couldn't stop her body from tumbling in the surf a few months ago, how that day put a stop to her dreams of traveling the world as a pro surfer. "Maybe I need a couple more weeks to build up my strength."

Drew opened the bag of food and retrieved a metal thermos and two mugs. "How about we have some soup and just enjoy an afternoon of no studying for you and no orchestra rehearsal for me. We could take a walk on the beach after we eat and sit by the fire until late tonight."

"Actually, I have to work on a paper for my women's lit class. I need to reread *Mrs. Dalloway* and finish my paper by next Thursday. Plus, I've got a lot more research to do."

Maddie reached into her backpack to retrieve a book of essays about Woolf and opened it to where she'd bookmarked a chapter on *Mrs. Dalloway*. She pulled out the bookmark with the

Wordsworth quote—the one Ally had given her a few years ago. Now tattered, the bookmark was a painful reminder of what they had once shared. Right after Maddie's surfing accident, Ally had abruptly cut things off. No apology. No explanation. Nothing. Over the past few months, Maddie thought about Ally a lot, but she too made no effort to reach out to her. What would be the point? Ally had made her choice. And so had Colin, for that matter.

Drew poured some hot and sour soup into a mug and handed it to Maddie. "I would think reading a novel once would be enough to get plenty of information to write a paper."

Maddie sat at the picnic table and took a sip of warm soup. "Reading anything by Virginia Woolf once is never enough. I need to go through the book and find quotes to support my analysis." After a couple more slurps of soup, she no longer shivered. Mom's hot and sour soup always warmed her, but this batch had way more chili paste than usual. The tangy and spicy flavors made her eyes water and her nose run.

Drew scooted closer to Maddie and draped his arm around her shoulders. "Knowing you, I bet you've already got most of the paper written. What's the paper about anyway?"

Maddie wondered how much she should reveal to Drew about her topic and whether she could adequately explain her focus. Even though the paper was due in a week, she was still formulating her ideas, but she decided to be vague about the controversial subject she chose for her paper. Maddie shrugged. "It's typical women's lit stuff. I'm mostly focusing on the main character, Clarissa Dalloway, and her inner struggles. I've got the intro and two body paragraphs written, but I still need to do a lot more research. I'm sorry I'm being such a dud. Just one more week of classes, and I won't be preoccupied with my assignments."

Drew slipped his hand in Maddie's. "You're not a dud. Look at me with rehearsals or concerts six nights a week. At least we have this afternoon to enjoy the beach. Hey, I heard Colin is transferring to USC. One of our buddies from the surf team told me yesterday morning when we were surfing."

"What?" Maddie stared back in shock. "Colin got into the University of Southern California? I thought his plan was to stay in Orange County."

"He got picked up to play basketball for USC."

This was the first Maddie was hearing about it. She and Colin did sometimes work the same shift at Royal Palace, but they rarely talked about anything other than work. Maddie would cringe any time she heard him talking to Ally on the phone. He was oblivious to Maddie's pain. "Figures he'd go to a college up in L.A. When does he leave?"

"Sometime next month. He's been going up to L.A. a lot to talk with the coach and attend some of the practices."

"I guess this means I'll probably pick up a couple more shifts at the restaurant." As she thought about Colin and Ally living in the same city, Maddie's jaw went rigid, and her eyes welled up with tears. She quickly put on her sunglasses and took a deep breath. The crisp ocean air soothed her and brought her back to the here and now. "We'd better eat the rest of the food before it gets too cold."

When Maddie peered inside the paper sack, she recognized Mom's banana pudding, but she wasn't sure what was sealed in aluminum foil. She pulled back the foil and caught a whiff of the savory flavor of vegetarian spring rolls. She dipped one of them in the sweet plum sauce and brought it to Drew's mouth. Maddie dipped a roll in the sauce and devoured it in only a couple bites. Though no longer piping hot, it was still crunchy and flavorful. Within minutes, Drew and Maddie ate all six spring rolls and finished the last bit of hot and sour soup.

Maddie crumpled up the foil and shoved it into the bag. "I'm fine if you want to surf for a while. I just don't think it's a good idea for me yet. Besides, I don't know what I was thinking to bring the surfboard I rode when I had my accident. I should've gotten rid of it and brought one of my older boards. It's gonna take me a while to get to where I was before."

"I think you're more ready than you think." Drew gently touched her arm and leaned over to kiss her on the cheek. "I'm gonna go get my surfboard."

While Drew went to his truck, Maddie tossed a couple logs into the fire pit and closed her eyes as she listened to the waves breaking on shore. When she opened her eyes, she found the sun had broken through the clouds. Only an hour until sunset, rays of amber light filtered through the grey clouds and cast golden flecks on the ocean. The wind had died down a bit, so there were fewer whitecaps. Though mushy, the waves didn't seem as powerful.

When Drew returned, he had a board wedged under his arm and another one in a surf bag slung over his shoulder. As he got closer, his beaming grin was impossible to miss. Then Maddie saw it—a huge red bow on the surf bag.

After Drew unzipped the surf bag, he pulled out a shiny new white surfboard and leaned it against the picnic table. "I know you said you're not ready to surf yet, but I'm hoping this'll change your mind. I had it custom made from a guy in San Clemente who shapes boards for many of the top surfers in Southern California."

Totally taken off guard, Maddie's eyes widened as she ran her hand along the smooth side of the board. The top was decorated with an intricate design—a black and white image of a giant octopus with its tentacles stretched across the board. "Wow, this is…amazing."

"I would've had Kai shape the board, but I wanted this to be totally different than the ones he's made for you. He's the one who told me about the shaper in San Clemente. Everything about this board is made to fit your body and your ability as a surfer. It's got a thin layer of wax on it, just in case you're up for trying it out right now."

Maddie kneeled in the sand. The body of the octopus and the tentacles covered the top part of the board where she'd lie when she paddled into the surf. Not sure what else to say, she fought back the tears as she admired the artwork.

Drew sat on top of the picnic table and furrowed his brow. "I chose the octopus because they're one of the smartest animals in the sea. They're fierce, just like you. I also read how an octopus can adapt to all sorts of conditions and can camouflage itself when it feels threatened or when it wants to hide. It can avoid potential dangers because it blends into its surroundings."

"I don't even know what to say." Maddie set her hand on the intricate design.

"The octopus also has the ability to bounce back after any sort of bad experience. If you'd rather wait and try the board in a few weeks, that's totally cool."

Maddie stood up and dusted the sand from her knees. She wrapped her arms around Drew and kissed him on the lips. "It's perfect, but I'm guessing this board cost a lot of money. It's bad enough that you never let me pay for anything when we go out."

"You're my girl. I want you to feel special. Let's just call it an early Christmas present."

"How am I gonna top this gift? I figured I'd just get you some new surf T-shirts and a cool beach towel." Maddie sat next to Drew and nudged him in the shoulder.

Drew always made Maddie feel special, and she was touched that he'd had a custom board made for her. She was concerned, though, if this meant they'd now reached a different level in their relationship—one that involved a deeper commitment and physical intimacy.

Drew leaned over to kiss Maddie and held her hand. "If you're really okay with me surfing for a while, I'm gonna get in my wetsuit and ride a few waves before it gets dark."

Maddie studied the incoming waves and looked at the fierce octopus on her new surfboard—the eyes looking directly into her own. "Seems kinda sad for me to not try out the new board. I think as long as I can get past these shore breakers, I'll probably be fine."

Once they got into their wetsuits, Drew and Maddie walked to the water's edge. As Maddie took a few more steps into the ocean, she again assessed the surf conditions. Her heartbeat increased, and her breathing became unsteady. Without much more thought, she hopped on the board and sliced her hands through the water. Though cold, the water invigorated her.

But after only five minutes in the water, Maddie became exhausted. The muscles in her arms and shoulders burned. When a small wave headed her way, she clung to the board and dipped under the wall of water. The breaker caused her to teeter on her board and fall into the whitewash. For a moment, she flailed her arms and gasped for air. Though weak, she managed to climb back on the surfboard and again tried to stroke her hands through the water to reach the surf zone, but she didn't have the energy to get past these small breakers.

Out of breath, Maddie looked behind her to see she was still close to shore. The muscles in her arms and shoulders were even more painful now. She sat atop her board and called out to Drew. "I can't make it to the surf zone! I can't even paddle past these small breakers." Tears streamed down her face, which turned into deep sobs as Drew paddled closer.

After Drew situated his board next to Maddie's, he sat up and reached over to set his hand on her leg. "I know you're frustrated that you don't have the kind of strength you had before your accident, but eventually you're gonna be just as strong. You'll see. I bet by summer you'll be competing again."

Maddie couldn't stop crying. Her shoulders heaved as she sobbed. "I don't see how I'll ever be able to compete…if I can't even make it to the surf zone."

"We're gonna take this one day at a time, okay? I bet within a few weeks, you'll be much stronger. If you're not up for this today, we can head back to shore and warm up by the fire pit."

Maddie splashed some water on her face—the ocean water mixing with her tears. She situated herself on the board and faced toward the breakers. "I don't want to head to shore yet. I think if I just take it slow, I'll make it to the surf zone."

"How about you hold on to my leg and let me paddle us both out to the waves? Just rest on your board and let me do the work."

Although she couldn't calm her breathing, Maddie gripped Drew's calf and let him haul her out to the surf zone. Drew probably assumed the tears were due to her frustration at not being able to paddle out to the waves on her own, but Maddie knew otherwise. How could she not feel the sort of love for Drew that he deserved? Maybe in time, she'd be adaptable just like the octopus and could love Drew as much as she once loved Ally.

The waves in the surf zone were smaller than they looked from shore. As a breaker headed their way, Drew got into position. Within seconds, he popped up on his board and rode the wave almost all the way to shore. Alone with only the gentle sound of the waves breaking, Maddie sat atop her board. She took a deep breath and gazed at the sunlight streaming through the clouds.

A few yards away, a wave started to form. The closer it got, the taller it became. Maddie assessed the approaching wave and prepared to dive below the whitewash, but at the last second, she positioned her back to the wave and sliced her hands through the water to try and tap into the energy of the breaker. Once her board caught the momentum of the wave, she stood and got used to the feel of the new board.

Though she didn't have the strength to zip down the face of the wave or ride the curl, Maddie rode the whitewater for a few seconds then moved her feet forward and angled the board to gain more speed. Exhilarated to be back in the ocean, Maddie couldn't stop grinning as she rode the wave all the way to shore.

On the beach, Drew hooted and raised his arms in the air as Maddie hopped off her board. Though the waves still called to her, she knew her limits. Now that the sun was about to set, she figured she and Drew would snuggle by the fire. After Maddie dunked under a small tumbler, she set her hand atop her board. She ran her fingers over the octopus and examined the intricate design once more. Maddie understood that she'd need to stay camouflaged for a while longer—at least until she got a better sense of what she wanted.

Chapter Fourteen

Wales, UK: June 2001

The lush green hills of the Welsh countryside, bright blue sky, and the deep azure of the sea sped past as Maddie gazed out the window of the car. She'd already taken dozens of photos in the past half-hour, most of the images likely fuzzy and obstructed by the windshield, or windscreen, as she'd learned to call it. Her first year of college behind her, Maddie was in Wales for the Virginia Woolf conference and wanted to see and do it all.

There was a perfect surf spot forty miles from the University of Wales, Bangor. Another conference attendee, Dot Campbell, was happy to make the drive, wanting to enjoy the Welsh coast herself. She didn't even mind that Maddie's rented surfboard could only fit in the car by being wedged between the front seats and nearly obstructing the gearshift.

Dot was an artist living in California but originally from England. She was attending the conference as an independent scholar, a term Maddie learned meant someone not involved in academia but interested in studying Virginia Woolf.

"What's the beach where we're headed called again?" Dot took a swig of cola then reached into a bag of cheese and onion potato chips.

"Porth Neigwl, or Hell's Mouth." Maddie checked the directions she'd printed out. "Looks like it's right off this main road. It's supposedly one of the best surf spots in Wales with four miles of sandy beach and grassy dunes."

"Sounds lovely. Care for any crisps?" Dot held up the bag.

"No, I'm fine." The overpowering odor of cheese and onion made Maddie feel a bit queasy, so she lowered the window a couple inches and inhaled the fresh air. "Did Woolf ever go to Wales?"

Dot licked the salt from the tips of her fingers, crumpled the bag of crisps, and tossed it behind her seat. "I'm not exactly a seasoned Woolf scholar. Only been to one other Woolf conference besides this one. I reckon she might've gone to Wales sometime in her life, but you'd be better off asking one of the Woolf experts once we get back to the university."

Maddie was excited for the opportunity to learn all she could while at the conference. She didn't have much of an academic background in Woolf studies, but so far, she'd learned quite a bit. However, she was well-read enough to recognize that the title of the conference, "Voyages Out, Voyages Home," was in reference to *The Voyage Out*, Woolf's first book.

With the rolling hills on one side of the road and the wide expanse of the sea on the other, they passed signs identifying the names of towns and streets. After three days in Wales, Maddie found she was checking her pronunciation guide less often. Maybe someday she'd take a proper class to learn how to read and speak Welsh. Up ahead, a placard indicated they were nearing Pwllheli, one of the towns leading to Porth Neigwl. When the car-sickness didn't subside, Maddie lowered the window a couple more inches and inhaled the sea air. No matter if she surfed in Southern California, Hawaii, or Wales, the smell of the beach always soothed her.

Dot smiled and looked at the narrow road ahead. "Haven't been to Wales in ages. Not since I was a child, way before I moved to the States. I reckon I was only twelve the last time I saw this gorgeous coastline."

Maddie took another photo of the rugged coast. "It's so different than the beaches in Southern California. I really appreciate you taking me to these beaches."

"Ah, it's nothing. It's our own little voyage out. I've got my easel and paints with me. I can easily spend a few hours painting the sights along the Llŷn Peninsula while you surf."

They passed through a town called Abersoch. Maddie craned her neck to see past the houses and hedges and to get a sense of what the waves were like. Her quick glimpses only revealed small sailboats and kayaks in the flat bay and lots of beachgoers on the sand. Perhaps Hell's Mouth would have better conditions and fewer people.

Maddie took a couple more photos, then slipped the camera into her backpack. In the side pouch of the bag was a print-out of an email from Drew that he sent a couple days ago. Full of heartfelt sentiments, the email left Maddie feeling uncertain and confused, but she knew Drew was waiting for an answer to his question.

"I feel bad you're gonna miss the keynote speaker today."

Maddie bit her lower lip and watched the scenery zip past.

"I got my fill of Woolf scholars yesterday. Besides, we've still got a day and a half of panels and the banquet tomorrow night. Might as well have a day of fun." Probably at least twenty years older than Maddie, Dot seemed hip and a bit rebellious.

"Missing a full day of panels makes me feel like I'm playing hooky from school."

"How often can you say you went surfing in Wales? I think we oughta hit a pub before we return to the university and get some fish and chips or bangers and mash. I bet we can find a pub with plenty of ales on tap. You're at least eighteen, right?"

"I'm nineteen. Back home, my mom's always harping on me to never drink, but I wouldn't mind trying some sort of ale while I'm in the UK."

"Well, here you're legal, so we oughta go have a coupla drinks after spending the afternoon at the beach."

A couple of drinks? Maddie hadn't ever had more than a couple sips of Drew's beer when they sat by the fire pit at the beach. She felt so free here in the UK. She could go to a pub and drink legally, she could stay out as late as she wanted, and she could skip a full day of the Woolf conference.

"So, how'd you get into Woolf?" Maddie asked, curious to learn more about her new friend. Since the carsickness seemed a bit worse, Maddie kept her eyes on the road and lowered the window again.

"You all right, hon? You look rather peaked."

"Just a little carsick, I guess. Or maybe the English breakfasts aren't agreeing with me. Not used to so much food in the morning."

"Won't be much longer in the car. Ah, so how I got into Woolf was that I discovered her by way of her sister Vanessa Bell, a Post-Impressionist painter in the early twentieth century. The more I studied Vanessa Bell, the more fascinated I became with the Bloomsbury Group."

"I wouldn't mind being part of something like the Bloomsbury Group. It's fascinating how people of varying backgrounds supported each person's creative endeavors." Maddie had read about the Bloomsbury Group for one of her classes last semester and learned they were a group of intellectuals and artists. When she first got to the conference, she doubted herself and wasn't sure if her limited knowledge of Woolf's books would allow her to hold her own during conversations, but she found that everyone was welcoming and encouraging, regardless of their formal education.

Dot hummed and tapped her hand on the gearshift while she sped down the road. "Members of the Bloomsbury Group definitely had a good thing going. Not only did they encourage each person's intellectual pursuits, but they also accepted each member, no matter their sexual orientation or background."

"Yeah, no one seemed bothered that Virginia Woolf and Vita Sackville-West were lovers."

"Right, despite both of them being married to men. I tell ya, even though we're now in the twenty-first century, way too many people are so fucking uptight and repressed. I don't give a shit what people think of me or my art. How about you? When did you first discover Woolf?"

After she considered Dot's question, Maddie decided to be bold and upfront. "A girl I had a crush on was really into Virginia Woolf. I guess I wanted to feel close to Ally because she read books by Woolf. All throughout high school, I read some of Woolf's novels because Ally had read them. Didn't realize it at the time, but that's when I first fell in love with her."

"Woolf or Ally?" Dot gave Maddie a sideways glance and bellowed out in laughter.

Maddie laughed as well. "Ally…and Woolf too, but obviously in an academic sense."

Sure that she was blushing, Maddie hoped Dot wouldn't look her way to see how nervous she was. She'd never admitted to anyone that she'd been in love with Ally.

Dot lowered the volume on the radio and slowed down when the road curved. "I'd say that's a mighty fine reason to become interested in Woolf. You were quite lucky to be aware of your sexual orientation at such a young age."

Maddie stared out the window, not sure how to go about explaining her complicated situation. She had a boyfriend back home; friends and family saw them as totally committed to one another—a boy and a girl who very much appeared as a normal straight couple. But after several months of no contact with Ally, they'd recently started talking again. Ally had surprised her with an email out of the blue, asking how she was doing and if she was surfing again. It had been two weeks before Maddie had replied, and only because Ally wrote again to say she'd broken up with Colin. They'd since exchanged a few more emails and phone calls, with Ally initiating each one.

Ally had invited Maddie to meet up with her in Paris with her family next week at her grandparents' summer home. Instead of the reconnection with Ally making Maddie happy, it made her feel more confused about Drew.

Dot drummed her fingers on the steering wheel. "I don't know about you, but this little trip to the coast will probably be the highlight of my vacation. Well, besides seeing my sister in London day after tomorrow."

"I'll be in London, too, and then I'll head to Cornwall to surf for a few days." Maddie got another whiff of the briny air. The adrenalin began pumping as she envisioned being in the water soon.

"If you'd like, I could give you a lift to London. I've got a helluva long drive. Took the train to Wales but rented this car to drive back to London. I'd hate to make that drive alone."

Taken aback by Dot's generosity, Maddie calculated how much money she'd save by not having to take a train to London. "If you don't mind, I'd be extremely grateful for the ride. I can help pay for gas."

"They call it petrol here, hon, but really, no need for you to pay for that. I'm just happy to have the company on the long ride. I'd offer you a place to stay in London, but Laura, my sister's partner, is a bit fussy about who she allows in her home overnight. Besides, you'd probably be more comfortable at a hotel. Laura gets home late most nights from work. Forty-two years old, and she's still bartending at a gay bar in Soho." Dot pursed her lips and furrowed her brow.

"What does your sister do?" Maddie hung onto the words "who she allows into her home" and was intrigued by the reference to a gay club in Soho. When she'd searched online for surf spots in Wales, Maddie also looked up gay and lesbian bars in London—at least to once and for all alleviate her curiosity while she was in the UK.

"She's a dental nurse. A decent profession for a forty-one-year-old, don't ya think? Don't know how Caroline ended up with someone who thinks bartending is a respectable career for a woman in her forties. At any rate, I'll be glad to drop you off in London before I head over to my sister's place. Maybe we can meet up one day to walk around Bloomsbury and see where Woolf used to hang out. Whereabouts are you staying?"

"At the Cardiff Hotel right by Paddington Station. How far is Soho from Paddington?"

"Depends on how you get there. By bus it'd be pretty fast, and by Tube, I reckon it's only a few minutes away depending on which line you take. You definitely should wander around Soho. Lots of great lesbian bars and cafés. You should go to the place where Laura bartends. It's more of a mixed bar, but I'm sure you'll see lots of lesbians there. Laura will take good care of you."

"Yeah, I'll check it out." Dot's suggestions were intriguing. Here in the UK, Maddie didn't have to reveal too many details of her life back home and realized she could do nearly anything she wanted while away.

After they passed through a residential area, Dot slowed down to enter a car park next to the sea. Huge waves broke a few yards off shore. Eager to hit the surf, Maddie waited patiently while Dot parked the car then took her easel from the trunk, or the "boot" as the Brits called it.

Maddie headed to the beach with her backpack slung over her shoulder and the surfboard wedged under her arm. Dot set up her easel a few paces from the parking lot, and Maddie dropped her things nearby on the sand. The nausea hadn't entirely let up since they got here, but the fresh air would hopefully settle her stomach before she went in the water.

Maddie studied the rough surf for a few minutes and waited for three sets to make their way to shore before she got into the wetsuit. Though she'd surfed in a variety of conditions, this break was new to her. It was far better to first see how the other surfers handled these waves. Although she rarely burned in the sun, she had no idea if the Welsh sunlight was stronger than it was in Southern California, so she reached in the side pouch of her backpack to retrieve a tube of sunscreen. Along with the sunblock, Maddie also took out the email from Drew. By now, she'd pretty much memorized the entire message. As she'd done often in the past couple days, Maddie reread Drew's heartfelt words:

You've only been away for a couple days, but I miss you a lot.

While you see the sights, know that I'll be thinking about you every day. So, to follow up with my proposal the other day when we were out in the water, I'd like to say it now in writing: Drew F. Richards can't wait to have Maddie J. Fong as his wife, to love, honor, and cherish her for the rest of his life.

Maddie stared at the stark black words on the white page—sentiments from a guy who'd likely make a great husband. Now a senior in college and getting ready to apply to graduate school, Drew no longer seemed like the kid she knew from the high school surf team. Suddenly, they were young adults and no longer teenagers. Grown-up responsibilities loomed in the near future: graduate school for Drew and three more years of college for Maddie.

Although she knew what the rest of the email said, Maddie skimmed the words once more:

I know we're both young, but I know I want to spend the rest of my life with you. I knew this long before we started dating and way before I kissed you for the first time. Whether you'd want a big wedding or something really small, I think it'd be pretty cool to hear people refer to us as Mr. and Mrs. Drew Richards once we said our vows and did all the other wedding ceremony stuff. I know the other day you said you wanted to think about it before answering me and that you thought you were too young to make such a big commitment, but know that I'll patiently wait as long as necessary...Love always, Drew.

The waves surged toward shore. Though Maddie adored Drew's sweet demeanor, sometimes his old-fashioned ideals grated on her. But did she love him? Did she enjoy their time together? Did she feel cherished and loved? She knew the answer to each of these questions was a definite yes. But did she want to spend the rest of her life as his wife? Did she want to be locked into a life of being Mrs. Drew Richards? Though she knew Drew would encourage her to pursue graduate school and a career in teaching, Maddie remained uncertain and confused about whether she wanted to be his wife. Or to be anyone's wife.

How simple Drew was to think they'd get married and live happily ever after. But maybe he and Maddie could have a good life together—a simple and normal life.

After she folded the email and slipped it into her backpack, she zipped up the wetsuit and put on the booties and gloves and walked to the water's edge. The man at the surf shop who'd rented Maddie her supplies said the water was usually around eleven degrees Celsius this time of year. That was fifty-two degrees Fahrenheit. Maddie shivered as the frigid temperature seeped through the booties and thick wetsuit.

Waves continued toward shore at a steady rhythm. Maddie took a few more steps into the icy water. She glanced behind to see how far she'd trekked from the dry sand where Dot stood at her easel. Maddie studied the swell for a couple minutes. Small tumblers washed over her legs as she took a few more steps closer to the surf zone. Once up to her thighs, she lay atop her board and headed toward the huge breakers. This was new territory for Maddie—a perfect time for her to explore this surf break.

For today, Maddie knew she didn't have to provide an answer to Drew's question, nor did she have to think much about it until she got back home. Yet at the moment she couldn't get a Woolf quote from the book *Night and Day* out of her head: "I really don't advise a woman who wants to have things her own way to get married."

Surely things were much different today than they were in the early twentieth century for women, but could Maddie have things her own way and still marry Drew? Here before her was a new surf break to experience—an opportunity for her to do what she most loved and not think about marriage proposals or happily ever afters. Later this evening, she'd get drinks with Dot, and in a couple days she'd wander the streets of Soho. Maybe her time in the UK would be her own voyage out, a time for her to put all curiosities to rest before settling down with Drew.

Maddie put all of these thoughts aside to paddle straight into a breaking wave. She dipped the front of the board under the frothing wall of water. When she emerged on the other side, she opened her eyes to see another breaker towering over her. This one jostled her body and flipped her off her board. The undertow sucked her body into the churning wave. Once she emerged, she gasped for air. When she looked to shore, she saw nothing but whitewash. Though these waves weren't that big, they carried a punch when they broke.

Determined to not get caught inside, Maddie got back on the surfboard and sliced her hands through the whitewater until she was out of the dangerous zone and in the line-up for the next set. She sat atop her board, and it struck her how far she'd drifted from shore—and how far she was from home. Though thrilled to try a new surf break in another country, Maddie longed for the warm Southern California ocean temperatures and predictable swell. She also missed being in the water with Drew. But here in the UK, she experienced a different break and new challenges. The newness of it all was exhilarating.

The crest of a wave was forming, so Maddie paddled with all her might until her board caught the momentum of the breaker. Not accustomed to wearing booties, it took her a moment to get her feet in the right position to control the board. Once she got comfortable on the surfboard, she surfed down the face of the wave and went aerial for a few seconds until she dipped back into it. With the surging whitewater under her board, she shot through the barrel and rode all the way to shore.

The first wave of any surf session always energized her. Eager to catch another one, she paddled through the surging whitewater to return to the surf zone. Proud she'd conquered Hell's Mouth, Maddie felt so alive and free. With another couple weeks left of her vacation, she had a feeling there would be many more firsts.

Chapter Fifteen

London, England: June 2001

The front steps of the Cardiff Hotel were worn but welcoming. Maddie leaned against the black, wrought-iron railing next to a planter of pink peonies as she studied a London guidebook. She located Soho on the map of streets and Underground stations, circled it, and got a sense of how she'd get there later.

While in this amazing city, she wanted to see it all—the parks, the locations where Virginia Woolf's novels took place, and the spot where she and Vita Sackville-West had fallen in love. This city would bring to life the words Maddie had spent years studying. This morning, she would experience the same route that Clarissa Dalloway traversed and go to Westminster.

Although it'd be faster to take the Tube, Maddie opted to stay above ground and make her way to Westminster on foot. It'd be her own little pilgrimage through London until she reached Soho this evening—the area she'd been longing to visit, a place where she knew she'd be comfortable.

Maddie slipped the guidebook into her back pocket and made a quick jaunt across the road. She rounded the corner and followed the street until she caught a glimpse of the lush trees of Hyde Park, an area close to Woolf's childhood home. A red phone booth near the entrance to the park reminded her she'd only called Drew once since she'd arrived in the UK. Since it was two in the morning back home, he would be sound asleep right now. Maybe she'd call later today? Then again, she'd also sent him a postcard and emailed a few times.

She'd also emailed Ally but hadn't yet received a response. Maybe Ally didn't have reliable internet access? Still, she'd be in Paris for a couple more weeks. It would be easy to take the Chunnel to Paris to see her. Maddie considered doing that instead of taking the train to Cornwall to surf. She and Ally had always had fun whenever they hung out. But if she went to France, she'd end up having to hang out with Ally and her family and probably not get any time alone with her. Besides, that old flame had long since died. Ally had made that clear. No, today Maddie wouldn't call Drew or contact Ally. Today, she was unattached and did not belong to anyone. Maddie lifted her chin, walked right past the phone booth, and entered Hyde Park.

On the left was a walkway leading to a huge fountain and ornate statues; to the right were dirt paths cutting through a grassy field with rows of giant trees. In her favorite Quiksilver T-shirt, baggy jeans, and running shoes, Maddie was ready for a few hours of walking, even though she felt a bit queasy this morning—probably from another big English breakfast. But she was excited about being out all day and not returning to her hotel until late tonight. If it got chilly this evening, she had Drew's favorite blue flannel shirt in her backpack to keep her warm. He'd stuffed it in her bag without a word, and she'd only discovered it on the plane.

Maddie chose to follow the paved path next to the fountain, which took her to a narrow lake called the Serpentine. The lake provided for a pleasant stroll and ended at another juncture with several trails and thoroughfares. Instead of staying on the paved walkway, Maddie traipsed through a woodsy area. Tall sycamores and huge oak trees provided ample shade while she hiked along the trail—very different than the palm trees and sandy beaches in San Clemente.

After Maddie left the woods, she ambled past manicured beds of bright flowers and cascading trees. She left the park and followed the signs to Buckingham Palace. Hundreds of people stood outside the tall iron fence as they watched the changing of the guard. Maddie pushed her way through the crowd to get a glimpse of Buckingham Palace.

Woolf had painted an accurate picture of this great London landmark in *Mrs. Dalloway*. But today's tourists were starkly different than the poor London citizens mentioned in the novel, despite both groups waiting outside the palace with hopes of a glimpse of royalty. Maddie watched the ceremonial procession for a while until she tired of the crowds. Today, she didn't want to be a tourist. She wanted to blend in, to feel like she belonged here.

Maddie made a detour down Hyde Park Gate to view Woolf's childhood home where she took several photos. For the next few minutes, she walked along the perimeter of Hyde Park until she reached St. James Park—the same park where the characters in *Mrs. Dalloway* relaxed on benches or ambled down the walkways. She knew she was near Westminster when she heard the bells of Big Ben striking—the same gongs Woolf described in her novel.

After the first bell sounded, Maddie counted the other thunderous clangs. Two…three…four…five…twelve gongs rang out just as she reached Westminster.

Near Westminster Abbey, Maddie sat on a bench under a shady tree and retrieved *Mrs. Dalloway* from her backpack. In the middle of the book, she'd bookmarked a page using the letter Ally had left in Maddie's high school locker a couple years ago. The note was full of broken promises and foolish sentiments. Though she'd pored over this letter numerous times, she hadn't read it in a long time. How silly these words seemed now after so much time had passed since they last kissed:

Even though we just saw each other a few hours ago, I can't wait to see you again. I never imagined that kissing someone could be so great. I love the way your lips are so eager for mine. I love that what we have is our own little secret, but the way I feel about you reminds me of something Coleridge said in one of his poems: "Place your hand upon my heart. Feel how it throbs for you!"

There was a time when Maddie would set her hand on Ally's chest and feel the beat of her heart. Her skin had been warm and the beat steady. The kisses they'd shared filled her with delight and left her wanting more. Now, the memory made her shudder. She slipped the letter back into the book and spent nearly an hour rereading passages from *Mrs. Dalloway* that she'd recently high-lighted: Details of the flower shop where Clarissa Dalloway bought the flowers for her party. Images of St. James Park. Descriptions of Big Ben and Westminster. Details of the passion-ate kiss Clarissa shared with Sally.

Maddie referred to these scenes when she'd written her paper on repressed sexuality—still a controversial subject these days. Her family and Drew had been lukewarm in their support, except for Kai. In her paper she'd argued that Clarissa had conformed to twentieth century heteronormative standards by marrying Richard Dalloway, suggesting that she stifled her bisexual tendencies and embraced a respectable life of being Mrs. Richard Dalloway.

Although the kiss in *Mrs. Dalloway* seemed impulsive and fleeting, Clarissa often reminisced about that moment. Woolf described Clarissa's world turning upside down when Sally kissed her. Though Drew's kisses were sweet and passionate, and Ally's were soft and sensual, Maddie never thought of them as exquisite. Maybe one day a kiss would turn Maddie's world upside down.

When she returned the book to her backpack, Maddie pulled out Drew's email and focused on the words at the end:

I'll patiently wait as long as necessary.

Thousands of miles away, Maddie need not give Drew an answer today. Or even next week. For the rest of the day, she'd carry on as if she didn't have a boyfriend back home who loved her and who'd likely be a caring and dedicated husband.

But sitting here in Westminster, Maddie had one of those thunderclaps of reality hit her: She had been, and always would be, attracted to women. And she would never be able to ignore that attraction. Her breathing became shallow, and her hands shook as she secured the email in her backpack. She couldn't stop smiling. This was her truth.

Drew's proposal could wait. Maddie zipped her backpack and resumed her exploration. There were still a few hours left in the day until she went to Soho—a place where she would likely fit in and could be anyone she wanted to be.

A brief stroll toward Westminster Bridge led her past an outdoor café and then to a tourist kiosk where she searched through a rack of postcards. Though she'd already sent Drew one postcard from Wales, she thought he'd enjoy receiving one from London, so she went through the rack until she found the right one—an image of the Thames at sunset with Big Ben in the background. She also found a few others that showed various London locations.

After Maddie paid for the postcards, she headed to Westminster Bridge. Midway across the bridge, she stopped and gazed at the Thames for a few minutes. The sun cast her shadow in the ripples of the water—the image blurry and distorted. From there, she moved on to Big Ben and stood under its shadow as tourists nudged past her. It was now a little after five o'clock. Back in California, Drew was likely packing up his surf gear and heading to the beach to surf like he did most mornings during summer. Maddie wondered how the waves were today, whether there was a south swell building, and if the surf had picked up.

She paused outside a phone booth and again considered calling Drew but reminded herself that for today, she'd carry on as if she wasn't attached to anyone.

On the other side of the bridge, she collapsed gratefully on a bench under a huge leafy tree. Even though she'd been in the UK for over a week, she still experienced waves of jetlag late in the day. Her feet ached from walking for hours through London. This was a good moment to rest and write a postcard. She flipped through them until she found the one for Drew. She pulled out a pen from her bag but found her mind was blank. Usually prolific, right now she didn't even know how to start this note. Maybe the photograph of the golden streaks of the setting sun reflected on the Thames would provide inspiration.

And it did. This image wasn't right for Drew, but it was perfect for Ally. Maddie laughed suddenly to herself as a burst of forgiveness filled her heart. Her anger at what Ally had done last summer dissipated, and Maddie wanted to at least connect with her on some level. Though she knew they'd never recapture what they once experienced, she was hopeful they could salvage their friendship.

Maddie dug through the side pouch of her backpack until she found Ally's address in France. Inspiration struck, and she wrote quickly.

Before long, most of the postcard was filled with her tiny, neat writing. Maddie skimmed what she wrote and added a bit more at the end:

You'd have a blast here taking photos of the amazing sights. The image on this postcard reminds me of some of your photos. To say I wish you were here is an understatement. There have been so many things I've seen and done that I wished I could have shared with you.

Though the last two sentences might be too much, she figured she didn't have anything to lose. At one time their bond seemed unbreakable. Maybe at this point, things could be mended enough for them to have some sort of a friendship.

From the other side of the river, Big Ben gonged once more. Ready to leave the touristy area, Maddie slipped the postcard into her backpack and made her way across the bridge. Out of stamps, she'd have to buy more on Monday.

Hungry for dinner and ready for a drink, she picked up her pace as she neared the Underground station. Her heart thudded hard as she thought about going to Soho and stepping foot inside a gay bar. In the UK, without her mother's strict rules and without a boyfriend at her side, Maddie could do whatever she wanted and be whoever she wanted to be. Practically running now, she whooshed through the entrance to the Underground and studied the map to figure out the fastest route to Soho. At this point, it was imperative that she get there as soon as possible.

Chapter Sixteen

Maddie stepped out of the Tube at Oxford Circus Station and followed the swarms of people heading toward the exit. It was exciting how people in the Underground stations never stopped, how hundreds of bodies merged onto the platform and funneled down the corridors to make their way to nearby theatres, bars, and restaurants. Exhilarated to be part of this energy, Maddie joined the crowd and made her way toward the escalators.

In front of her, a man held another guy's hand, and two girls around Maddie's age exchanged a quick kiss when they stepped onto the escalator. Thrilled to see such openness, Maddie checked out some of the women who brushed past her but quickly averted her gaze when any of them looked her way.

Halfway up the escalator, Maddie noticed a young blond woman a couple steps behind her. She had cropped hair and tattoos, and when she smiled at Maddie, Maddie smiled back as her stomach fluttered and knees became weak. In a tight, low-cut white tank top that accentuated the woman's large breasts, the blonde looked fit and very attractive. When the girl scanned her eyes over Maddie's body, Maddie's excitement grew, but so did her terror. Lots of guys had checked her out at the beach, but no one had ever looked at her this way. Not even Ally.

At the top of the escalator, Maddie blended in with the horde of people but peeked behind her to search for the girl. All Maddie saw was the back of her cropped hair as she darted across the street and merged with the crowd. Disappointed that the blonde was so far ahead, Maddie followed Oxford Street for a few minutes as she took in all the sights of Soho—rainbow flags displayed outside pubs and cafés, pink triangle stickers affixed to windows, and lots of lesbian couples walking hand-in-hand down the street. A sign in front of an internet café caught her eye: "Free internet usage with any food or beverage purchase." Without hesitation, Maddie pushed the door open and approached the counter.

"What'll you have?" a tall man behind the counter asked without looking up from his laptop.

"An iced vanilla latte." Maddie set a few coins on the counter and tossed some loose change in the tip jar. "If I want to use a computer, do I need some sort of access code?"

The coffee machine whirred as the guy started to make Maddie's latte. "Each computer is already set up for fifteen minutes of free internet usage. If you want more than fifteen minutes, you gotta pay extra. It's five quid for an hour of internet."

Once her latte was ready, Maddie took it to a nearby computer where she quickly logged into her email. While she took a few sips of iced coffee, she scrolled through an email from Kai and one from the International Surfing Association verifying her registration for a surf competition in the fall. But then she saw what she was hoping to see—a response from Ally. Maddie leaned forward and skimmed the email:

So glad to hear you got to surf in Wales! It's cool that you can now officially call yourself an international surfer. Paris is an amazing city. So far, I've been to the Louvre and to the Musée D'Orsay. This museum used to be an old train station and is located right next to the Seine. Being away in France has been great, but it's also given me time to think. Well, specifically about us.

Maddie stared at those two words: about us. Her heart thudded hard as she read the next few lines:

Even though we're both in different countries right now, I like that you're not that far from me. I've missed you so much. Here I am in Paris taking in all the amazing sights while you're over there in London. We'd be crazy to not meet up since we're only a short train ride away from one another. I'm hoping you're able to take the Chunnel over to Paris to see me. It'd be nice to finally talk about some things that have been on my mind and to say things I should've said months ago. It just seems better to talk in person rather than to say it in an email.

What could Ally possibly need to talk about? Was this a long-overdue apology?

Plus we'd have fun seeing the monuments and checking out the galleries over here. In a few days, we're driving to Normandy and Mont Saint-Michel. If you don't mind putting up with my mom's bad French, you could come with us. Maybe you could even surf in Normandy. So, if you can pull yourself away from London for a couple days, we could sightsee together in France. Hope to see you soon...Ally.

Though the lines about needing to talk were rather cryptic, everything else in the email sounded ordinary and platonic—exactly how things were when Ally insisted on keeping their relationship a secret. Although relieved that she and Ally were now friends again, Maddie wasn't sure what to write in response. With just a couple minutes left of free computer usage, Maddie only had time to type a few words:

It's great to hear from you! Surfing in Normandy would be cool. It'd be fun to hang out and see the sights. I'll check to see if I can switch some things around to be able to make it to France while you're there. I've missed you, too.

Maddie stared at the last line of her email, her finger hovering over the backspace tab. She took a deep breath and then hit send. After she took a couple more sips of iced latte, she left the internet café and walked briskly down Oxford Street until she found Berners Street. Before leaving the U.S., Maddie promised Ally she'd take a few photos of the place where Coleridge once lived in London. Though she'd only taken one British literature survey course at Chapman University, Maddie had learned Coleridge was way more complex than Ally ever conveyed.

Maddie only needed to take a few paces down Berners Street to find the round blue plaque up high on a big building:

SAMUEL TAYLOR COLERIDGE
1772-1834
POET AND PHILOSOPHER
lived in a house on this site 1812-1813

The sidewalk across from the building was the perfect place for a wide shot. Maddie took a few photos and then zoomed in to get a more focused image of the plaque. A wave of sadness washed over her. It would have been so special to have seen

Coleridge's house with Ally.

The street was surprisingly empty of cars, so Maddie paused halfway across to quickly snap a couple more photos. Though her amateur photographs were likely poor quality compared to the ones Ally took, these few snapshots should be sufficient.

Once she reached the sidewalk, she took one more photo and leaned against a phone booth with a bunch of stickers and advertisements affixed to the door. Right at eye level, someone had taped a two-lined Coleridge poem to the window. This was not unusual in London. Dead poets and authors still had many fans who trekked to their birthplaces or homes to leave memorabilia or odd personal items. Though she wasn't familiar with this poem, it pretty much summed up Coleridge's love life—and her own, to some extent:

To meet, to know, to love—and then to part,
Is the sad tale of many a human heart.

Maddie smiled sadly. An intense longing for Ally washed over her, but despite the latest email, what the two of them had once shared was now merely a bittersweet tale. Tempted to peel the poem from the phone booth and give it to Ally when they met up, Maddie instead took a couple close-ups before tossing the camera into her backpack. Hungry for dinner, she backtracked down Berners Street and followed Dean Street until she reached the bar where Laura worked.

But she didn't go in.

She paced outside the bar several times before making herself stop. She leaned against a mailbox and wrung her hands. Was she really about to do this? A group of people exited the bar, laughing and chattering away—a reminder that if she was uncomfortable, she could simply leave. Resolved to at least get a bite to eat, Maddie took a deep breath, wove through the crowd, and stepped through the entryway.

The place was packed with a few guys and lots of women— most of whom were young, fit, and boyish. She nudged past a few raucous partiers and joined the queue of people lined up at the counter to order drinks. Maddie reached the counter as a buff bartender filled a glass of beer from the tap. She got his attention and leaned forward. "I'm wondering if Laura is here tonight. I'm a friend of her sister-in-law's. I'm here from California."

"Hang on, I'll go get her." The man walked away to speak to the female bartender at the other end of the bar.

She set down a plate of fish and chips in front of a customer and approached Maddie. "You must be Maddie. I'm Laura. Dot said you'd probably stop by."

"My plan was to come by last night, but I got pretty tired by early evening."

"Sightseeing in this city makes most people knackered. I heard you enjoyed surfing in Wales recently. Must take a lot of guts to surf in a place like that. This your first visit to London?"

Maddie laughed quietly. "Actually, it's my first trip to Europe…and, the first time in a place like this. Took me a while to get up the nerve to walk inside." Though she'd only just met Laura, she was surprised at what she'd admitted. Tonight was about letting go and finally venturing into a gay and lesbian bar. Admitting the truth to Laura, a complete stranger, was part of that. But why did it make her feel like her heart was going to beat out of her chest?

"Well, ya picked a great place to hang out tonight. The DJ's likely to start playing music soon. What'll you have, love? We've got a pub menu here on the counter, but maybe you'd like a drink first?"

"I guess I'll have a Strongbow and a cheese toastie if you have that." For nearly every night for the past week, whenever she ate in a pub, she ordered the same thing: a cheese toastie, the closest thing to an American grilled cheese sandwich. Maddie leaned against the counter to watch Laura fill a glass from the tap. When she and Dot had gone to a few pubs in Wales, Maddie tried a couple different ales but discovered she preferred hard cider over ale. Stronger than most beers, one pint of Strongbow made her pretty tipsy.

Laura set the cider on the counter. Maddie took a quick gulp and perused the bar. Worried she stood out as noticeably American or too feminine to belong in a place like this, she thought about how different she looked compared to the other young people. For now, she'd stay in the corner of the bar and hopefully blend in. Fortunately, tonight she wore baggy jeans and a flannel shirt over her T-shirt and only wore mascara and a hint of eyeliner.

Laura placed a plate of food in front of Maddie. Tired and hungry from all the walking she did earlier, Maddie finished half the sandwich in a matter of minutes. From the dance floor nearby, loud music pulsated from the speakers, and a few people started to dance.

Be it the effects of the alcohol or the exhaustion from walking for so many hours, the dancers mesmerized her—especially those who pressed their bodies close together. Maddie rested her head against the wall next to the bar and gazed at the women around her. Maybe she'd venture into a different bar soon, someplace not as noisy and chaotic. Or maybe she'd go back to her hotel and go to bed early.

While Maddie tried to make a decision, a tall, curvaceous brunette entered the club. Way more feminine than most of the people here, she had long brown hair and carried herself with grace. Dressed in a tight black miniskirt and a matching jacket, she walked with confidence and poise. Maddie watched her every move. The high-heeled woman strutted through the crowd and found a seat at the far end of the bar.

Laura set a plate of French fries in front of Maddie. "These are on the house."

"Thank you." Maddie gave Laura a smile. So she'd be staying a little while longer, then.

"You ready for another cider?"

"No, I'm good. I'm still working on this one." Maddie bopped her head to the beat and noticed that the tall woman waved a hand to get Laura's attention.

"Be right back. Looks like the dame has summoned me. Gotta make sure I get her martini just right." Laura rolled her eyes and went over to greet the woman.

While she sipped her cider, Maddie watched the dame through the mirror behind the bar and witnessed how she interacted with others. Or how she attempted to interact. Any time she spoke to someone, no one gave her the time of day. Laura seemed bothered to have to take her drink order.

Maddie finished her cheese toastie and ate most of the fries. She crumpled her napkin and placed it on the plate. The dame continued to sit there by herself. She seemed too perfect to be in a place like this—overly theatrical and debonair in the way she held herself. Laura placed a martini in front of the woman. Most of the people in this bar drank beer. At least Maddie fit in by drinking something amber in a tall glass.

Maddie glanced at the dame, only to be startled when Laura reached over the bar to retrieve her empty plate.

"You see something you like?" Laura set the dish behind the counter.

Not sure how to respond, Maddie shrugged and averted her eyes. The thudding bass from the music pulsed in her chest; her ears rang from the loud voices of people shouting nearby. Although the bar was filled with lots of young women, Maddie was captivated by the tall brunette a few feet away.

Laura used a rag to wipe the counter and glared at Maddie. "Trust me, love, this one's not your type. Best you stay away from Alex. A quick hello will turn into a gabfest. She'll talk your ear off. Just stay put and not even make eye contact with her."

Maddie was perturbed that Laura would even think she was here to hook up with someone. "Why do you think I have a type?"

"I reckon you haven't quite figured that out yet, but my guess is Alex isn't anywhere near what your type might be. If you'd like, I can keep your bag behind the counter in case you want to dance later."

Maddie handed her backpack to Laura, relieved to be free of it for a while. Although she knew she surely didn't have a type, Maddie couldn't stop admiring how curvaceous Alex's butt looked in her tight dress and how the high heels made her legs look so shapely. So far, everything about this trip was about new experiences—about living like an independent adult. However, she still felt like her mother's teenage daughter who had curfews and rules to follow.

Maddie decided to say hello to Alex.

Up close, Alex's ruddy complexion, fine lines around her eyes, and dark age-spots on her hands made it clear she was older than she appeared from a distance. Still, Maddie was determined to be bold while in London and say hello. Nothing wrong with making a new friend.

Maddie plopped down on the barstool next to her. Alex's dark, big hair was perfectly styled. Her shadowed and lined eyes, her creamy skin, and her plum-colored lips were all done up with such perfection. But something about Alex seemed different. The jaw seemed a bit too chiseled, the hands too big. And the hair was a wig. Alex was not a woman. At least not born that way. Even more intrigued now, Maddie was compelled to be in the presence of this person—to learn why they came here dressed this way.

"Great shoes," Maddie yelled over the thud of bass from the dance floor.

"Thanks, darling. They're Givenchy," Alex said over the din.

Maddie nodded, even though she had no idea if Givenchy was an expensive line of footwear.

"I'm Alex." She held out a hand. "Short for Alexandra."

"I'm Maddie, short for Madelyn." Maddie shook Alex's hand and caught a glimpse of her chest and wondered how a man could've created such a voluptuous décolletage.

Alex took a dainty sip of her martini. "Are you on holiday here?"

"Yes, for another week and a half. It's been fun being on my own this whole time."

Alex stared at Maddie for a moment and glanced at her clothing. "My guess is you're from California."

"How'd you guess? The baggy jeans and surfing logo T-shirt?"

"Mostly your accent. I spent a lot of time in L.A. years ago when I was in film. What part of California? And what's a young girl like you doing in London by herself?"

Maddie's Southern drawl had long since disappeared, but she had no idea she sounded like a Californian. Though proud that she now sounded like any other young person from California, sometimes she was a little sad that she had far fewer ties to Mississippi. Maybe someday she'd go back and finally meet her paternal grandparents. "I live in San Clemente, a coastal town between L.A. and San Diego. I came to the UK for a literature conference, but I'm planning to check out the beaches in Cornwall soon to surf. I've got a surfing competition coming up in a few months."

"Ah, a surfer girl. You'll find Cornwall to be quite lovely this time of year. Not too many gay or lesbian bars there, though."

Although the focus of Cornwall would be to fit in as much surfing as possible, it only now dawned on her that London would be her only opportunity to hang out in gay bars. There was also another factor to take into consideration. "Before I go to Cornwall, I might take the Chunnel to Paris. My friend Ally is there. Haven't seen each other in a while. It's been weird to be away from her for this long."

Alex leaned closer and set a hand on Maddie's arm. "Is Ally your lover?"

The physical contact and bold question flustered Maddie. "Um, no, she's not my lover. I have a boyfriend back home."

How strange that word sounded to her: lover. What Maddie and Ally had at one time could hardly be described as being lovers. It didn't even feel right to call Drew her lover. He was her boyfriend, a guy who cherished her despite her poor attempts at being an affectionate girlfriend. They'd only recently started having sex, but she never considered him her lover. Before they became intimate, Maddie understood that sex could bring two people closer. So far, that hadn't happened for her, but maybe in time she'd feel more passionate about Drew.

"A boyfriend? Then what's a girl like you doing in a place like this?" Alex bellowed out in laughter and slapped her manicured hand on the counter.

"I didn't want to get hit on by guys at a regular club, so I figured this'd be the safest place for me. The last thing I wanted was to have to ditch some guy in a straight club. Plus, I really like the music here." All of this sounded like total bullshit after it came out of Maddie's mouth, but she didn't feel like explaining how complicated things were for her right now.

"Well, dear, I've ditched a few guys myself." Alex grinned and picked up her drink.

"Do you frequent this bar often?" Maddie took another sip of cider. Nearly finished with her pint of Strongbow, she felt floaty and relaxed from the alcohol.

"I've been coming here every Saturday night for the past couple years."

Maddie and Alex exchanged a few cordial words for a few minutes, and then the DJ shifted the beat to hip-hop tunes. When a Missy Elliott song came on, Maddie bopped her head to the familiar beats and glanced again at Alex's Givenchy shoes. She admired Alex's bravery for going out dressed this way—so flawlessly tailored in women's designer clothing. Not to mention the smooth and soft skin, without even a hint of stubble. Much different than what Maddie expected to see on a man in drag. She'd only seen drag queens on TV, but maybe Alex was transgender? Feeling sheltered but curious, Maddie had so many questions to ask.

"What originally made you decide to come here…as Alexandra?" Maddie finally asked, worried her question was rude, but the effects of the alcohol made her uninhibited in what she said.

Alex leaned in closer—close enough that Maddie could smell a spicy perfume. "I was probably not much older than you when I used to dress this way at home. But only in the privacy of my bedroom. It gave me such a thrill to wear dresses and heels, but I was afraid to go out in public that way. Took me nearly thirty years to finally feel brave enough to go out this way."

After she calculated Alex's approximate age, Maddie felt sad that it took her so long to go out in public this way, how she kept that part of her life secret for much too long. "So, you live life as a woman? I mean, all the time?"

"No, dear, only on Saturday nights and special occasions. In my usual life, I wear a suit and tie like most men."

"Excuse me for being so blunt, but do you prefer to be called *she* when you're dressed this way?"

"When I'm Alex, I'm flattered when people use the female pronoun, but I'm used to the male pronoun in my usual everyday life. I sometimes go out with women dressed this way, sometimes with men, but I have no plans whatsoever to transition or live life as a woman. For the most part, I fancy both men and women."

"So, you're…bisexual?" Tipsy and a bit woozy, Maddie felt awkward saying that word aloud. She'd never used it except when writing literature papers or during class discussions when referencing Virginia Woolf and Vita Sackville-West, or Clarissa Dalloway and Sally Seton.

"Darling, I refuse to put a label on anything, especially my sexual orientation. But, truth be told, I do get a thrill when a man or a woman finds me attractive, regardless of their own sexual orientation. I'm a far cry from a ladyboy, but I find that too many people are compelled to put a label on other people. Why not just love whoever you want to love or fuck whoever you want to fuck?"

Although Alex's choice of words was shocking, her openness was admirable. It was liberating to converse with someone so daring and with whom Maddie also shared some similarities. "I can see why it'd be flattering for a woman to check you out. At least that's how it feels for me." Maddie laughed softly, proud and thrilled that she admitted this out loud.

Maddie caught a glimpse of herself in the mirror behind the bar. Alex's painted face, the big wig, and the tailored outfit looked starkly different next to Maddie's simple appearance.

The door to the bar opened, sending a shock of cold over Maddie's skin. The air was thick, heavy with summer rain. Through the door walked the girl she saw earlier on the escalator. The blonde looked even more intriguing now in the dim light of the dance club.

Alex raised her martini and clanked the glass on Maddie's. "Well, surfer girl, you've already made my Saturday night so much better. I'm glad you ventured into this bar tonight. Does the California boyfriend know you're here?"

"He has no idea I'm in a place like this. He's actually hoping to call me his fiancée, but I haven't said yes to his proposal…or no. I'm not even sure I want to stay with him." Maddie tried to steady her breathing as she thought about what she'd just admitted to Alex.

"This gets more interesting by the minute. You here to sow your lesbian oats before settling down with this guy?"

"I guess I was just curious to come to a few gay bars while I was in London. I feel like I can't move forward with Drew if I didn't come here to check this out."

"Darling, nothing wrong with exploring that curiosity. Took me nearly thirty years to finally feel brave enough to go out in public like this. Times were so different back then than they are today. For years I was secretive about going out in drag. Even my wife had no idea."

"You're married?" Maddie listened attentively but kept a close eye on the dance floor through the reflection in the mirror behind the bar.

"Not anymore. We were married for nearly twenty years, but I kept my secret the entire time we were together. About midway through our marriage, I started to meet up with guys every now and then. But I adored my wife. Finally told her I was drawn to men, which absolutely shattered her. For a while, we tried to make it work because we still loved each other, but we both realized it'd never work."

Maddie thought about what Alex said as she finished the last of her cider and turned to search for the cute blonde. Right away,

Maddie spotted her leaning against the mirrored wall next to the dance floor.

"So, do you love this boyfriend back home? I mean, enough to marry him?" Alex nudged Maddie.

"Drew is an amazing guy. He's sweet, attentive, and kind. I do love him, and I think we could have a good life together. I guess sometimes I just feel too young to settle down with someone, and I do wonder…about certain things." Like all the times she kissed Ally, how she always wanted to explore her body and experience what it was like to make love with a woman, but they'd never gone that far.

"No need to rush things."

With only ten days left in the UK, Maddie still had a lot to explore—and so many questions left unanswered. "Were you scared…the first time you went out in public as Alex?"

"It was utterly thrilling." Alex threw her head back and laughed softly. "But it was terrifying, too. We fear what we most want, but without fear, it wouldn't be worth pursuing."

"How'd you get past the fear to finally go out in public this way?"

"In early 1999, I'd been frequenting a placed called The Admiral Duncan, a predominantly gay establishment. I went there a few times a week to scope it out. I mean, as a guy in male clothing. Finally, one Friday night in spring, I made my debut as Alexandra. Being in the bar dressed as a woman felt absolutely liberating, but a week after I'd gone there in drag, I heard the bar was hit by a nail bomb. Three people killed. Many more injured. The papers said a neo-Nazi was the culprit."

Maddie gasped, and her hand flew to her mouth. "That's awful! I'm so sorry."

Alex slowly nodded, all the laughter and joy gone from her face. "Thank you. It was. I didn't feel safe to go back there, in drag or not. I still don't. You'd think this would be an era of acceptance, a time when people like us would be fully welcomed."

Maddie paused at "people like us" and clasped her hand on Alex's. "This seems like a pretty safe place, right? I mean, I feel welcomed here, even if I'm just here to check things out."

"Or be checked out."

"I'm being checked out?" When she turned around to peruse

the near vicinity, Maddie felt a rush of excitement.

"Darling, loads of women here have noticed you, including the blond cutie you keep eyeing over by the dance floor." Alex's smile had returned.

Embarrassed that Alex had picked up what she'd been trying to hide, Maddie laughed. "Nothing wrong with being curious, right? I saw her earlier at the Tube station and was excited to see her come in here."

"That's Erika. She's on summer break from university. Comes here a couple times a month. Broke up with her girlfriend a while back. I reckon she's on the prowl."

Erika was currently observing others in the bar but stayed by herself next to the wall.

Maddie kept her eyes on Erika. "I'm not here to meet anyone. Just here to have a good time."

"Darling, I've got a lot more years on you, so I might be coming from a totally different place, but I think someday it'll be more than a curiosity for you. It's not a matter of if, but when. Just don't wait thirty years like I did."

Maddie didn't want to wait thirty years. She searched for Erika on the dance floor, considering whether she should join her. However, since she was exhausted, she was content to remain perched on the barstool for the rest of the night. Maybe she'd walked too much today or still had some remnants of jet lag. But would jet lag still affect her on her eighth day here?

"I'd say it's about time you go ask her to dance." Alex waved to Laura behind the bar. "It's Saturday night. Might as well enjoy yourself. Perhaps explore that curiosity a bit?"

Not sure how to respond, Maddie stared at her hands on the counter, the fingers interlaced. Still woozy from the cider, she took a few deep breaths and hoped the nausea would pass.

"Another round?" Laura asked.

Before she had a chance to say no, Maddie heard Alex say she wanted to buy her another cider and then headed to the loo. Flattered that someone wanted to buy her a drink, Maddie figured she'd take a few sips but not finish it. She sat on the barstool and moved her body to the steady beats, reminiscent of how she used to get lost in the sets the DJ played at high school dances. Two places where Maddie felt confident were in the ocean and on the dance floor—her body feeling at one with a wave or the beat of a song.

When Laura set the drinks on the counter, she leaned close to Maddie. "Alex isn't bothering you, is she? She means well, but sometimes she's a bit much."

"No, she's not bugging me." Maddie took a sip of cider and noticed Erika ordering a drink from the other bartender.

"I reckon that one's more your type than Alex," Laura said and winked.

Maddie's eyes widened, and her heart raced at the comment. Was that true? She didn't respond to Laura, but instead watched Erika, trying not to stare too much at the way she subtly moved her body to the music as her petite hips and shoulders grooved to the beat. When Erika leaned against the counter, Maddie enjoyed the view of her cleavage and the intricate tattoos on her chest and arms.

Erika got her drink from the counter and approached Maddie. "I saw you at the Underground a little while ago. Probably should've talked to you on the escalator, but I didn't want to come across as being too forward. I'm Erika."

"I'm Maddie. I heard this bar was the happening place for gays and lesbians in London. Figured I'd check it out." Maddie cringed at how silly her comment must've sounded, but Erika's steel blue eyes captivated her. After another slurp of cider, she searched the crowd to see if Alex was on her way back to the bar.

"The better lesbian bars are a couple blocks away. So, you're American," Erika said, her voice curious yet playful.

"Yes, from Southern California. Been in the UK for a little over a week now. I started my trip in Wales where I went to a literature conference and then headed down here to London. Had to check out the dance clubs while I was here. I was stoked when I heard the DJ playing hip-hop just now." Though tipsy, Maddie took a couple more sips of Strongbow.

"Maybe you'd want to join me tomorrow night at a different club, a place that plays way better music." Erika reached behind the counter to grab a pen, instigating a disapproving look from Laura, then wrote her number on a napkin and jotted down the name of the dance club and the location. "I'll be there around nine. Sundays during summer don't get hopping until late."

Erika took another swig of beer and excused herself to go to the loo. Maddie slipped the napkin into her back pocket as another bout of wooziness hit her. Probably best to stay still until it passed. That was what Maddie meant to do, but then the DJ played a remix of Annie Lennox's "Little Bird" from the 1990s. She and Ally had danced to this song at one of their high school dances, becoming one with the music and one with each other. Maddie closed her eyes, lost in the thump of the bass.

But midway through the tune, Maddie could no longer keep her body still. She took a sip of Strongbow, slid off her seat at the bar, and headed to the dance floor. Fueled by cider and mesmerized by the words to the song, she closed her eyes and swayed to the rhythm. While lots of other bodies were moving around her, Maddie was in her own world—a place filled with sweet memories of dancing with Ally.

When Maddie opened her eyes, Erika was standing nearby and watching her. There was a look of longing in Erika's eyes that Maddie found thrilling. Even in the dim light, Erika's perky breasts stood out in that tight tank top. Without any hesitation, Maddie took Erika by the hand and guided her to the dance floor. Grateful this was an extended remix of "Little Bird," Maddie became even more lost in the song once Erika was next to her. Together, their bodies moved as one to the steady beat.

Erika's body pressed behind hers, and Maddie gasped. The feel of her breasts against her back was incredible. Erika slid her hands across Maddie's hips and then down her thighs; an intense heat traveled through Maddie's body. While she swayed to the thumping bass, she smiled when she heard the line about a little bird falling out of the nest and being free.

Maddie turned to face Erika and looked deep into her eyes. Eager to touch her, Maddie placed her hands on Erika's hips and pulled her closer—the heat surging through every fiber of her body. So alive and free right now, Maddie didn't want this song or this moment to end. Grateful she still had several days left in London, Maddie was determined to explore as many gay and lesbian clubs as she could. Here in Soho, she was free to spread her wings and fly from the nest.

Chapter Seventeen

London, England: June 2001

Maddie left Tottenham Court Underground Station a little after eight and made a quick jaunt down Oxford until she found her way to Dean Street. She wanted to find Candy Bar before it got dark. A few paces down the sidewalk led her to Carlisle Street where she searched for the bar. Not sure she was in the right area, she glanced at the napkin from last night while she wandered down the narrow road. Under Erika Chase's name was the address of the club. When Maddie got closer to the bar, her legs became weak, and her heart thudded hard as the nervousness overcame her.

The simple white and black exterior didn't seem all that exciting. If she hadn't known this was a dance club, she would've assumed it was a storefront and walked right past it. A few women hovered just inside the doorway. There was no music. Candy Bar didn't look or sound like a happening place. Maybe the club had a downstairs area where people danced?

This club was close to where Maddie hung out last night. She considered not meeting Erika and instead returning to the bar where Laura worked. Comfortable in that bar, she could have a drink and chat with Laura. Maybe Alex would be there tonight. Besides, Erika and Maddie hadn't made a definite plan to meet here; Erika's invitation seemed casual and noncommittal. Erika probably wouldn't even be fazed if Maddie didn't show up. But Erika looked really hot in that tank top, and Maddie had been very turned on when they'd danced.

With a few minutes until Erika would be here, Maddie leaned against a drainpipe outside the club and indulged in some people-watching. Two young women walked hand-in-hand as they crossed the street and approached the club. One of them had a buzz cut; the other had long dark hair that went down to her waist. Both of them wore black dresses and pumps.

Had Maddie chosen the right clothing for a place like this? Her favorite pair of ripped and faded jeans went well with the button-up black shirt and Doc Marten boots. Although Maddie had spent a little extra time doing her hair this afternoon and applied a bit of mascara and eyeliner, right now she felt plain and dumpy. She hoped her outfit would at least not make her look like a straight American teenager.

Standing by herself outside a lesbian bar wasn't helping matters, so she strolled down the street until she reached the corner. A sudden need to yawn hit her, and she paused on the sidewalk. Why was she so lethargic? She'd slept until eleven this morning and hadn't done much today other than wander through Hyde Park and get a cheese toastie and chips for dinner.

The upcoming meeting with Erika didn't help as thinking about it made her palms sweat and hands shake. Maybe it would be a good idea to return to the hotel at a decent hour, especially since she and Dot were planning to meet in Bloomsbury tomorrow morning.

But then she recalled Alex's words from last night: We fear what we most want. Certain that she didn't want to be in her fifties and still full of curiosities, Maddie headed back to Candy Bar.

It was now or never.

A group of women stood at the entrance—some of them boyish, others butch, a few of them feminine. Maybe she'd fit in after all. Maddie paced down the sidewalk as she searched for Erika. Maybe they were supposed to meet inside? Perhaps she was running late? How odd it was that her first real date with a woman was in a foreign country. But maybe this wasn't an actual date. Erika had simply mentioned she'd be at Candy Bar at around nine o'clock tonight. For all Maddie knew, Erika had planned to meet a bunch of friends and happened to invite Maddie.

Maddie took a couple deep breaths and then looked up to see Erika heading her way. She looked hot in a navy-blue tank top and jeans. Maddie's nerves transformed into total excitement.

"You came," Erika said then greeted Maddie with a hug. She pulled away and looked her over. "Wow, you look great."

"Thank you, so do you." Maddie smiled and nodded at the crowd hovered around the entrance. "This definitely looks like a fun club."

"Candy Bar is by far the best lesbian hang-out spot in London. They opened right about the time I came out, so I've got lots of great memories of this place. Wait'll you see the dance area." Erika smiled and slipped her hand in Maddie's.

So, this was definitely a date.

Now that it was dark, the pink neon sign above Candy Bar made this place look much more inviting. Music started playing from somewhere within, and it definitely had a good beat. Erika led them through the entryway until they reached the bar. Loud and chaotic, the club was full of all sorts of lesbians. And one look at the crowd reassured Maddie that she was indeed dressed appropriately.

Erika set a twenty-pound note on the counter. "What'll you have?"

Though accustomed to ordering a pint of Strongbow, Maddie figured she ought to branch out and try one of those ales Dot raved about on their last night in Wales. "If they've got London Pride on tap, that'd be great."

Erika ordered a London Pride for Maddie and a Guinness for herself, her head bopping to the rhythm of the music. After they got their drinks, Erika slipped her hand in Maddie's and led her to a dimly lit room with pink walls and dark hardwood floors. Once they found an unoccupied corner, Maddie set her beer on a table and sat atop a pink bar stool next to Erika.

Erika scooted her chair closer to Maddie and leaned forward. "So, last night you mentioned you were in Wales for a literature conference. Did you present a paper or lecture to an auditorium of students?"

Maddie laughed. "No, I'm not even close to being a literature scholar. At least not yet. I was at the conference to learn as much as I can about Virginia Woolf." She took a sip of beer, surreptitiously noting that though Erika's chest, shoulders, and arms were covered in tattoos, she had a softness about her that was intriguing.

Erika took a couple sips of Guinness and smiled. "You came a long way to go to a conference totally focused on Virginia Woolf. I reckon you must be a big fan of her to come all this way to hear people lecture about her."

Maddie cupped her hands around her beer and thought about how best to respond, trying not to let Erika's soft lips distract her. "A fan? I'm not sure that's the best way to describe it, but I'm fascinated by Woolf's writings and her life. One of my professors urged me to go to the Woolf conference and even arranged to have the registration fees covered by Chapman University, where I'm getting my bachelor's degree."

"I was never fond of writing term papers when I was in high school, but I always did enjoy reading books, especially the classics."

"Same with me. I always had my head buried in a book when I was a kid. Then when I was a bit older, I got into surfing and joined the surf team. So, I had to balance my love of books with my love of surfing." Maddie laughed softly. Though already a bit tipsy, she took another sip of beer. "How about you? Where do you go to school?"

"I'm in graduate school at the University of Birmingham. I'll have my master's in physiotherapy by next year and will hopefully do a physio internship somewhere in London."

"Graduate school? Wow, that's pretty impressive. Eventually, I plan on getting my master's in literature or maybe even my PhD. What made you choose physiotherapy?" Maddie leaned toward her, hanging on Erika's every word.

"Like you, I was a high school athlete except my sport was what you call soccer in your country and football here in the UK. I played it all throughout high school and again when I was at university. I always appreciated how the athletic trainers got me back in the game soon after I was injured."

"Same here. I've had my own share of physical therapy. Last year I was in a pretty bad surfing accident, but I was back in the water only a few months after the injury. Unfortunately, the scar on my face is a reminder of that awful day."

Erika leaned closer. "I wouldn't have noticed it if you hadn't said something. Glad you healed so fast from your injuries."

"Me too. Right now, I'm training for a big surf competition in the fall."

When Erika smiled, her entire face lit up. "Never met a competitive surfer. How long have you been surfing?"

"For about four years. It's taken me a while to get back to where I was before I got injured. Lots of intense workouts at the gym and in the water to get as strong as I was before my accident. Thought of giving up a couple times, but I kept at it and finally feel ready to compete again. I'm pretty busy with school, but I'm hoping to do a lot of competitions in the next few years."

Erika stared at her hands. "My mum's had lots of physio over the years," she said quietly. "Nearly five years ago, she was in a serious car accident and ended up with lots of mobility issues. It's always just been me and my mum, so when she was injured, I took a year off from school to care for her."

Maddie's eyes widened, and she put a hand on Erika's arm. "I'm sorry. That must be so hard to deal with. Sounds like you and your mom are close. Is she doing better now since the accident?"

"She's doing much better, but she still has some trouble getting around. When I'm on break from school, I stay with her here in London and help around the house. I learned a lot about how to help her based on what the carers taught me, but her accident made me realize I wanted to learn the proper way to care for people with serious injuries. Seemed like physio was the right field for me." Erika sat up straight and flashed her bright smile again. "How about you? Why'd you choose literature?" She took another sip of Guinness and leaned closer to Maddie.

Maddie laughed and fumbled with the napkin in her lap. "I guess you could say I got into literature because of a cute girl named Ally Flores. When I was in ninth grade, Ally turned me into a literature geek. Throughout high school, she used to read me love poems and passages of literature that described how she felt about me. And here I am, five years later in England for a literature conference. Always thought about doing a semester in the UK. Maybe I'll look into doing that next year."

"Sounds like a brilliant idea to me." Erika smiled and stared at Maddie for a moment. Something about Erika's steel blue eyes made Maddie want to talk to her all night long. "I'm glad you came here tonight. Wasn't sure you'd show up."

"Up until late this afternoon, I too didn't know if I'd show up." Maddie laughed and averted her eyes from Erika's as she drank the rest of her beer.

"If you're not busy tomorrow night, would you like to have dinner with me? I mean, in a place that's much quieter than this. There's a lovely restaurant by Putney Bridge with an amazing view of the Thames. We could take a walk along the river after dinner."

Maddie thought for a moment. She and Dot were planning to spend the day together, but she'd likely be free by early evening. "Yeah, I'd like that. Haven't seen that part of London yet."

Erika reached across the table to set her hand on Maddie's. "So, this Ally Flores. Is she still reading you love poems?" Erika's voice was playful yet curious, and there was a subtle look of longing in her eyes.

The question was a surprise, but Maddie knew the answer. "No, that's all in the past. Back in high school, we were both two innocent girls exploring our feelings for one another." It was the truth. So why did saying it out loud make her sad?

"High school, huh? I was a rather late bloomer. Didn't come out until I was twenty-two. So yeah, nearly five years ago."

"I was actually a little bit younger than that when I first realized I was attracted to girls. But, at the time, I was just a confused kid and not sure why I felt so drawn to a girl I'd met at camp."

"Wow, you were quite young to have a crush on a girl at that age."

Maddie laughed and shook her head. "She was actually one of the camp counselors and didn't have a clue that I had a crush on her. After I moved to California, we kept in touch for a while, but then when she got engaged to some guy, we lost touch. I hardly ever think about my first crush, but I guess in some ways, I'm still trying to figure it out."

Erika laughed and squeezed Maddie's hand. "I sometimes think we'll always be trying to figure things out. I don't know about you, but I'm ready for another drink and some time on the dance floor. After we left the bar last night and you went your own way, I couldn't stop thinking about how amazing it was to dance with you."

"Yeah, last night was definitely a lot of fun. I think another beer is a great idea." Maddie gave Erika a flirtatious smile and reached into her pocket for some money. "As long as you let me pay for this round."

They headed to the bar together. Maddie leaned against the laminated countertop, and Erika stood behind her and set her hands on her shoulders. They'd only met last night but were already so comfortable with each other. When Erika pressed her chest against Maddie's back and slid a hand down to her right hip, Maddie gasped in delight, and Erika laughed softly.

The bartender served them their drinks, and Maddie took a couple sips of beer as they moved through the crowd. Instead of returning to their place in the corner, they left the bar area and entered another room where the thudding bass got louder. The room was packed with women who moved their bodies to the music. Another few sips of beer rendered Maddie weak in the knees, but she enjoyed the buzz.

Once they set their drinks on a table next to the dance area, Maddie slipped her hand in Erika's and led her to the dance floor. Similar to last night, their bodies moved as one. Completely lost in the music, Maddie closed her eyes and became mesmerized by the steady beat. From behind, Erika pressed her body against Maddie's and set her hands on her hips and pulled her close. Her body heat made Maddie melt with a desire she hadn't felt in a long time. She loved the way Erika's body grooved with hers, how her hands found their way to her abs under her shirt.

After they danced for a while, they took a break and sipped their beers. Even though Maddie felt a bit woozy from the alcohol, she was stoked to be here with such a hot woman who was so attentive and interested in their topics of conversation.

Maddie's eyes traveled from Erika's soft lips to the intricate tattoos on her chest and arms. "How long have you had these tattoos?"

"I got my first one when I was eighteen and didn't stop until both arms were done. I've also got one on my belly. Hurt like hell, but it's my favorite tattoo." Erika raised her shirt to reveal some sort of flowering design on her lower abs just above the waist of her jeans. The intricate tattoo started a couple inches to the left of her belly button and continued down toward her hip.

When Maddie noticed the ripped abs, she let out a quiet gasp and reached over to run her fingers over the tattoo. "I think that's my favorite one, too."

"I've got more…in places I can't really expose out in public like this."

Erika's words made Maddie shudder with excitement. "I'm definitely glad I decided to come here tonight. Looks like you might need another Guinness." She smiled and slipped her arm around Erika's waist.

"I'm thinking a shot might be fun. You up for that?"

"Yeah, that sounds fun."

Even though Maddie had no idea what she'd be drinking, surely taking a shot of any type of liquor would be quick and easy. While she waited for Erika to come back with the drinks, Maddie drained her glass and watched as people danced and conversed nearby. She was so comfortable in London—and very content in this bar. But there was still more of England to explore. Once she returned home, she'd talk to her advisor about doing a study abroad trip in the UK. She'd have to give up surfing during that time, but living in England for a few months would be worth it.

The music got louder, and the pulsing base became more intense. Maddie grooved to the rhythm. A fit, young woman smiled at Maddie from across the room and nodded. Maddie smiled back. The woman wove her way through the crowd and approached her.

"I like how you move. You wanna dance?" The woman stepped closer.

"Oh, I'm actually here with someone." Maddie grinned, and her heart thudded hard. Overjoyed that someone asked her to dance, she bit her lower lip as the woman smiled then wandered back to the dance floor.

Two boyish girls around Maddie's age sat at the table next to her and kissed. A couple butch women walked past hand-in-hand. Maddie couldn't stop smiling. Everything seemed so clear right now, but something else occurred to her. She couldn't marry Drew. Not now, not even in a few years after she finished her education and settled into her teaching career. Her smile faded. Once home, she'd tell Drew that she couldn't be with him. Though she could easily call him or email him telling him she couldn't marry him, Maddie knew she owed him an in-person break-up. She wished she didn't have to hurt him in order to be true to herself and happy, but she knew she needed to be honest with him and end things.

Erika returned with four shots of some sort of amber liquor and set the drinks on the table. "I hope tequila is fine. I got four so I don't have to go back for more."

Without any thought, Maddie threw back the shot of tequila and slammed the glass on the table. The liquid burned as it went down her throat, and she coughed. Her head buzzed from the loud music, and her legs were weak. Too drunk to dance, she managed to find her way to the bar stool and sat down. Maddie cupped her face in her hands and leaned forward as she waited for the dizziness to pass.

"You okay?" Erika stood at Maddie's side and ran her fingers through her hair.

The touch sent shivers through Maddie's body. "I think I'm good with just one shot."

Erika downed a shot of tequila. "I reckon I might've been presumptuous by ordering you two shots."

The thumping music made Maddie feel even more woozy. "You wanna get out of here and maybe find someplace more quiet?"

"I had the same thought about an hour ago. Wasn't sure you had the same idea as I did."

"Oh yeah, I wanna see where that tattoo ends." Maddie brushed her hand against Erika's.

Erika gave her a wicked grin, downed the other two shots, and slipped her arm around Maddie's waist.

They made their way through the crowd and out to the street, found a secluded spot against a brick wall, and embraced under the night sky. The crisp air made Maddie feel less dizzy, and Erika's arms held her steady. She laughed, wild and free, and slid her hands across Erika's back and then down to her ass.

Maddie pulled back and looked deep into Erika's eyes. Erika gave her a slow, lazy smile that sent a shot of arousal straight through Maddie's body. She ran her fingers over the tattoos on Erika's chest and shoulders and pulled her closer, her eyes lingering on the luscious curves and softness of Erika's lips.

Erika gently set both hands on Maddie's cheeks and gazed at her. "I've been wanting to kiss you since I first saw you standing outside the bar."

Maddie moaned softly and moved closer to Erika. "That makes two of us." She couldn't hold back any longer, and their lips met.

One kiss quickly became many kisses, and their intensity increased exponentially. Erika's clever lips and wicked tongue filled Maddie's entire being with pure desire. Frenzied heat radiated through her body and settled between her legs. Maddie was meant to be with someone like Erika—someone who turned her world upside down. Though thousands of miles away from home, Maddie had never felt as comfortable in her own skin as she did right now.

Chapter Eighteen

Maddie snuggled close to Erika in the cab as Big Ben and the Houses of Parliament blurred past. She'd wandered around here yesterday, but she marveled at how magnificent these sites looked when lit up at night. Erika slipped her hand between Maddie's thighs and pulled her closer. Although not as tipsy now, Maddie barely remembered getting in the cab and riding through Soho, but her desire to kiss Erika and explore every inch of her body magnified as they made their way across the city.

Thrilled to experience London at night with such a hot woman at her side, Maddie set her hand atop Erika's. "You said your mom lives in Wadsworth? Where's that in relation to the central part of London?"

Erika clasped her hand in Maddie's and leaned closer to her. "It's Wandsworth, where I grew up until I left for university. It's a borough in southwest London, not too far from the Thames. How about you? You also live with your mum, right? Somewhere near the shore? Must've been nice growing up close to the beach."

"Actually, we live with Kai, my mom's boyfriend, and his elderly parents in a big house half a mile from the beach. I didn't move to San Clemente until I was fourteen, but I enjoy being in the ocean as often as possible."

"I bet you look great in a bikini." Erika's voice was playful and sultry, her words causing Maddie to shudder with excitement. She leaned over and touched Maddie's cheek, then pulled her closer for another kiss.

Maddie melted with desire and relaxed her body into Erika's. The kisses stopped when they crossed the Thames at Albert Bridge. Lights from buildings and homes reflected on the dark water coursing beneath them.

After they passed a huge park, they entered a residential area. Now on a street with rows of two-story brick houses, they pulled up next to a home with a flowering tree out front. Though dark, pink blossoms shone dimly on the branches—the last remnants of a spring bloom. Once the cab reached their destination, Erika clasped her hand in Maddie's as she opened the car door and led her to the sidewalk. Maddie caught a whiff of dank air—perhaps from the Thames only two or three blocks away.

Maddie staggered across the sidewalk and followed Erika down a narrow walkway and up a flight of stairs until they reached an upstairs flat. In the doorway, they kissed once more. Erika's lips were soft and eager—her tongue hungry for Maddie's.

Maddie couldn't get enough of her. No one had ever kissed her like this. No one had yearned for her the way Erika did.

There was a wheelchair in the entryway. Maddie pulled away from Erika's embrace. "You're sure your mom won't hear us?"

"Nah, she's sound asleep by now. Not much that'll wake her once she's taken her sleeping tabs and is sound asleep. You want a cup of tea? Maybe some biscuits?"

"No, I'm good, but I need to use your restroom. That beer's gone right through me."

"First door on the right." Erika waved an arm toward the hall.

After washing her hands, Maddie splashed some cold water on her face and tidied up her hair as best she could. Erika was waiting for her, and Maddie wanted to be presentable. Still a bit tipsy, she leaned on the basin and examined herself in the mirror, beaming at her reflection. This vacation had led her to places she'd never imagined exploring.

She returned to Erika, who greeted her with a sweet smile and a firm embrace. When Erika held her tighter, Maddie flinched and pulled back slightly. Though her breasts were usually somewhat tender right before her period, they were way more sore than usual.

"You okay?" Erika asked.

"Yeah, just thinking we should move to your bedroom."

"Great idea." Erika turned off the overhead light and led Maddie down a hallway into a dark bedroom.

After Erika clicked on a bedside lamp, she took Maddie's hand and led her to an open window. Though the view was some-what obstructed by trees and houses, the Thames was visible in the distance, the moonlight reflecting on its waters. They stood in silence, enjoying the peace of the summer night.

Erika stretched, revealing a few words tattooed on her inner forearm—a quote Maddie recognized from *Hamlet*. She trailed her fingers over each word. "When did you get this one?"

"I got it when I was twenty-two. 'To thine own self be true' seemed fitting once I finally came out. This quote sums up how it felt to no longer hide my true identity."

Erika smiled then ran her hands through Maddie's hair and kissed her softly on the lips. She guided Maddie to the bed. Full of longing, Maddie lay back and pulled Erika close as she lost herself in Erika's kisses. Though fully clothed, the heat intensified. When Erika moved her knee between Maddie's legs, her breath became shaky.

"I don't usually go home with—" Maddie started to say.

"No, I get it." Erika pressed her lips against Maddie's. "It's not customary for me to bring a girl home so soon after I meet her. It's just that…there's something about you that's so different than anyone I've ever met."

"You're sure it's not because I'm an American here on vacation and will be heading back to the states soon? You know, an easy lay with no strings attached?" Maddie's playful questions surprised her. She unbuttoned her shirt and wrapped her arms around Erika.

Erika laughed then kissed Maddie on the shoulder. Erika's lips followed Maddie's scapula and then traveled down to her breasts. "No, definitely not that. Besides, I think I recall you saying you'd like to do a study abroad session in the UK. It's not like you're only here for a summer holiday."

"It's gonna be hard to board that plane the week after next."

"At least you'll be back, right?" Erika set her hand on Maddie's cheek and kissed her softly. Soon, her lips found their way to Maddie's neck. Erika's tongue playfully flicked Maddie's earlobe.

The kisses sent shivers down Maddie's neck, and she moaned quietly. She wasn't sure how to answer Erika's question. Maddie bit her lower lip and gazed at Erika in the dim light. "I want to come back. I really do. I can't make any promises, though, but I'll definitely keep in touch and let you know. At least we have a few days until I leave."

"And a few more nights, including dinner tomorrow."

"So, a second date?" Maddie pressed her hips and pelvis against Erika's thigh.

Erika removed her tank top and kissed Maddie harder as she ran her hand down Maddie's leg. "Definitely a second date. And a third, and hopefully a fourth. My God, you're so hot. I can't wait to explore your body, then hold you all night long."

Erika's words made Maddie crave her even more. She rolled onto her side and slid her hand across Erika's hip and then down to her lower abs—her fingers blindly searching for that tattoo. Erika unzipped her jeans, and Maddie's hand moved lower until she found the soft patch of hair a few inches below her belly button. As Maddie touched Erika, electricity coursed through her own body and settled between her legs.

Maddie withdrew her hand to throw off her shirt and moaned as Erika ran her hands over her breasts and then down to her abs. There was a definite wetness between Maddie's legs, and she really hoped Erika's hands would travel lower. When Erika kissed her on the chest and then moved her soft lips to Maddie's belly, a burning heat radiated through her body.

"Wait," Maddie whispered as she struggled with the button on her jeans. "I have to—"

Erika's soft laugh was warm against her skin. "Need some help?"

"Maybe—no, got it." Maddie wiggled out of her jeans and tossed them on the floor. After a few more of Erika's burning kisses, she was ready for the next step. Maddie unclasped her bra and removed her panties. Now, after years of longing, she was finally skin-on-skin with another woman.

"You're gorgeous," Erika whispered. She quickly removed the rest of her own clothes. Jeans, bra, and underwear joined Maddie's on the floor, and Erika pulled her back into her arms.

Though she trembled and couldn't calm her shaky breaths, Maddie closed her eyes for a moment and traced her fingers across Erika's shoulders and then down her back. Erika moaned softly. Filled with passion and longing, Maddie pressed her body against Erika's, but she couldn't stop her body from shaking.

"You're shivering. I should shut the window," Erika said quietly.

"No, stay. Warm me up with your body." Maddie giggled and moved her body in rhythm to Erika's. Her sultry words surprised her, but she didn't want Erika to leave her side. Not even for a few seconds.

Maddie pulled back but only to run her hands over Erika's large breasts and erect nipples, looking deep into Erika's eyes while she did so.

Erika gasped and let out a satisfied sigh as her eyes glazed over in desire. "More. Please. I love the way you touch me."

Maddie's hand drifted down to the intricate tattoo on Erika's belly. Some sort of flowering vine, the tattoo started near the belly button and trailed over her hip and down her thigh. Maddie followed the vine with her fingertips all the way down the side of Erika's leg.

Erika squirmed at her touch and giggled as she guided Maddie's hand higher. "Wrong way."

Then she moved her hand to Erika's inner thigh and inched her way higher until her fingers brushed against her wetness. Erika's moan fueled Maddie's excitement, and they kissed again and again.

The feel of skin against skin made Maddie shudder with desire. Erika's tongue playfully flicked Maddie's nipple. The cool summer breeze chilled Maddie's bare skin. When Erika's lips traveled down Maddie's ribcage and found their way to her lower abs, an intense warmth radiated through her body. While Erika's lips and hands explored Maddie's body, the heat magnified. Maddie lost herself in Erika's gentle touch.

Erika slid her hand between Maddie's legs and ran her fingers over her slickness—something she'd always longed to experience with Ally. "Oh, my God," Maddie gasped quietly. Her breathing intensified. Though she'd only met Erika yesterday, Maddie let go of all inhibitions and slid her legs apart, giving Erika everything.

"You feel incredible," Erika whispered. One finger slipped up and down, then two. They rubbed back and forth in a steady pulse.

Maddie wrapped her arms around Erika's shoulders, part of her brain dimly registering that she should leave Erika's arm free to work its magic. "More." Maddie nuzzled her neck. "Please, more."

Erika laughed softly and added a third finger, increasing speed when Maddie's rapid breathing turned into high-pitched, breathy whimpering for more.

"You're close, huh?" Erika murmured in her ear.

It was impossible to speak, and Maddie hoped the "mmhmm" would be enough.

No one had ever touched her this way. No one had ever made

her this wet. No one had ever given her such clarity as Erika did right now. Erika didn't let up on the pressure—so gentle yet firm. She pressed a soft kiss to Maddie's lips and slid her tongue inside.

That brought her over the edge, and her entire being suffused with pure pleasure. Her body stiffened except for her hips, which bucked against Erika's fingers, and they were not slowing down, clearly determined to wring every last sensation from her. Maddie gripped Erika's arm and moaned over and over as the shudders subsided. She pulled Erika closer as the delicious fingers finally slowed, gliding up and down, then giving her a slow gentle stroke and pulling away.

Erika returned the hug and held Maddie back tightly. "Take your time," she whispered. "You let me know when you're ready for more."

Right now, everything was so right and perfect. And Maddie knew she was definitely returning to the UK soon. It wasn't a matter of if, but when.

Chapter Nineteen

London, England: June 2001

Maddie slumped against the wrought iron fence next to Tavistock Square Gardens, waiting for the queasiness to pass. She'd already thrown up earlier in her hotel room and had put it down to all the drinking last night. Getting back at six in the morning probably didn't help. Breakfast had been a piece of plain toast and some black tea. That had seemed to have settled her stomach, until now. Just catching a whiff of the food from the café across the street had set off the nausea again. It came over her in suffocating waves. She cursed under her breath as she tried to pull it together.

It was probably just a hangover. Maddie simply wasn't used to alcohol, and this was how all hangovers felt, right? She would enjoy her day in Bloomsbury with Dot and vowed not to drink anything other than soda during tonight's date with Erika.

But this trip was all about realizations, and another had made itself known: her period was three weeks late. Always regular, she usually got a period every twenty-eight to thirty days, but last week she assumed the jetlag and stress from traveling had something to do with being late. The mild concern had now turned into dread because it'd been nearly two months since she last had a period. Although she and Drew only had sex a few times, they hadn't always used protection.

When the nausea subsided, Maddie took a few sluggish steps down Tavistock Place. Maybe this was simply a hangover. She took a deep breath. Dot would show up at any moment. No matter what it took, Maddie was going to enjoy the day in Bloomsbury. It was thrilling to stroll in the same neighborhood where Virginia Woolf once walked. She took in the lush trees of Gordon Square and the plaque on the wall of a five-story building indicating where members of the Bloomsbury Group had once lived and worked.

When she heard Dot call her name, Maddie turned to see her friend dressed in an oversized grey Virginia Woolf T-shirt, black leggings, and bright orange Nikes. Dot looked eager and ready to power-walk through Bloomsbury and wander through the British

Museum. Maddie's heart sank. Despite her determination, she barely felt up for a slow stroll through the park, but she plastered a bright smile on her face when Dot got closer.

"Hiya, hon, looks like a great photo op to me." Dot pulled a camera from her canvas bag and took a photo of Maddie standing next to a bright red door with the Bloomsbury Group sign above her head.

After they took a few more photos, Dot and Maddie strolled along the perimeter of Gordon Square and caught up on what they'd done for the past few days. Although Maddie shared a few details about yesterday, she didn't mention anything about going home with Erika or feeling queasy—be it from drinking too much or from possibly being pregnant. That word seemed like such a foreign concept to Maddie. Though she saw herself as eventually having a child, she couldn't imagine it happening at such a young age. This had to be a hangover. She'd feel better as the day wore on.

They passed Russell Square and merged onto Montague Place, coming around the corner to Great Russell Street where they were greeted by the tall spired gates of the British Museum. Red double-decker buses idled in front of the museum as tourists filtered onto the sidewalk and up the steps.

Another wave of nausea hit Maddie at the entrance, and she stopped in her tracks.

Dot paused in front of the doorway. "You all right, hon?"

Maddie refused to let an upset stomach put a damper on her day. "Just tired from last night, I guess." But being inside the stuffy museum only made the nausea even worse. Maddie clapped a hand over her mouth and dashed to a nearby loo. Once there, she threw up the toast and tea from earlier this morning. Shaky and sweaty, she hung her head over the toilet bowl and waited for the queasiness to subside.

"Mad? You okay?" Maddie heard from outside the stall.

"Oh, shit," Maddie said under her breath, then felt her stomach heave once more. All she wanted to do was get back to her hotel as soon as possible.

"Perhaps a little too much booze last night?" Dot chuckled.

"Yeah, I guess I'm not used to drinking so much." Maddie wouldn't be able to handle a full afternoon of wandering through the British Museum, but she didn't want to disappoint Dot. Maybe she could sit outside on the steps while Dot toured the museum. "I'll be out in a moment."

"Take your time. I'll wait for you in the lobby, okay?"

"Okay." Maddie waited until Dot was gone before exiting the stall. She stood at the basin and splashed cold water on her face. Droplets rolled down her skin as she stared at her reflection in the mirror. This wasn't a hangover. She could no longer ignore all the signs: tender breasts, fatigue, missed period, and nausea. Thousands of miles away from home, Maddie wanted to figure this out on her own before she called Drew. She had to know for certain before letting him know.

As she stepped out of the loo, Maddie decided to tell Dot she was too tired to explore the British Museum, but Dot met her with an understanding and kind smile.

"My guess is this might not be a hangover. How late are you?" Dot asked softly.

"Three weeks." Maddie started to cry—deep, wrenching sobs that made her body shake.

Dot wrapped her arms around Maddie and stroked her hair. "Hon, you don't know for sure that you're expecting. But I thought you said you had a girlfriend."

Maddie pulled back from the hug and wiped her eyes with the back of her hand. "I never actually said she was my girlfriend. Ally and I were involved when we were in high school, but it was always something we kept secret. We never really reached girlfriend status. I've got a boyfriend back home. Been with him for about a year now, since shortly after I graduated from high school."

"Yeah, things didn't seem to add up on our trip to the coast. Plus, after having three kids of my own, I know the signs."

"I feel like such a loser." When Maddie looked at the people wandering past, she lowered her voice. "I'm a straight A student in college. I'm not the type of girl who gets pregnant at nineteen."

"Trust me when I say you're not the only studious girl who's made this kind of mistake. Let's get you outside, get some fresh air, and go from there. They've gotta have a Tesco or a Boots nearby. We'll have you wee on a stick and find out once and for all if you're pregnant."

Dot helped her out the door. Maddie kept a firm grip on her arm, all the way from the museum to the nearest pharmacy.

"You wait right here." Dot pointed to a bench outside the store.

"No, I'll buy it." Maddie stepped toward the door. "I gotta be an adult about this. I'm a grown woman."

"Not by much you are. You're still a kid, really. I've bought enough of these pregnancy tests to know where they're kept in stores like this."

Maddie waited for Dot, staring all the while at a red call box nearby. Should she call Drew to tell him the news? Or maybe she could not tell him and terminate the pregnancy. No one but Dot would have to know about any of this.

When Dot returned with a brown paper sack, Maddie started to tremble. With a surf competition coming up in September, she needed to continue training and moving forward in college. How would a baby fit into all of this? And how was she going to tell her mom?

"You wanna do this somewhere here in a public loo or back at your hotel?" Dot asked, her expression compassionate.

"I think I'd rather go back to my hotel," Maddie said quietly.

"I got you a bottle of Evian, the water with the highest level of bicarbonate. It always worked well for me when I had morning sickness. Also got you some crisps. The salt from those might ease the nausea a bit."

Maddie peered in the bag to see the pregnancy test—a blue and pink box with the words "quickest and most accurate" emblazoned on the package.

Once Dot hailed a cab, they rode through the city to the hotel. When the taxi idled at a stoplight, Maddie caught sight of the familiar red and blue sign of an Underground station. There were still so many more areas of London to discover. Would she still have a chance to explore more of England before she returned home? If the test came back positive, would her adventures be over? How different her life would be if she had a baby. No more surf competitions, at least not for a while. No opportunities to study in the UK for a semester. And no more chances to explore her curiosities.

But there was always one other option. No one back home would ever know about any of this.

"What's the fella's name?" Dot asked.

"Drew," Maddie said as the taxi idled in front of Regent's

Park. She peered into it as far as she could see—another area of London she'd yet to explore.

"You've been dating him for a while. Must be a special guy for you to stay with him for so long."

"Yeah, he's a great guy. Recently, he proposed to me. Haven't given him an answer yet. I'll probably need to make a decision pretty soon, especially now."

"Not an easy decision. When Peter proposed to me about fifteen years ago, I actually said no. Ran the other way and dated lots of other guys. Truth be told, there was more sleeping around than dating. You're probably learning way more about me than you care to know." Dot chuckled as she looked out the window.

Maddie laughed quietly, comforted she had a friend in the UK to go through this with her. "Well, look at me. Didn't think I'd have to tell a new friend I might be pregnant. I do love Drew. Just didn't think I'd need to give him an answer so soon. How'd you end up deciding to marry Peter?"

"After a couple years of dating around, I realized I'd let a good one go. Thought it was too late because I'd heard Peter had a new girlfriend, but when I phoned him one day to admit that I was a fool to say no to his proposal, he took me back without hesitation. I can't imagine not being with him. He allows me to pursue my dreams and goals and be my own person. Heck, he didn't even flinch when I told him I wasn't gonna take his last name when I married him."

Maddie considered what Dot said and thought about how Drew seemed so excited for them to be Mr. and Mrs. Drew Richards. But why not Drew Richards and Maddie Fong? Or, Maddie Fong Richards with no hyphen? She'd never seen herself as the type to hyphenate her last name once she married someone. "Seems like Peter doesn't hold on too tight and lets you have a lot of freedom."

"Yeah, I'm lucky. Look at me here in the UK for three weeks without him. He's back home taking care of the kids while I see the sights and spend time painting."

Another wave of nausea, although thankfully not as strong as the others, hit Maddie right as the taxi pulled up to the hotel. It was time to face reality.

Maddie paid for the cab, stood on the sidewalk next to Dot, and held up the crumpled paper sack. "It's weird how my life is going to be so different after I see these results."

Dot set her hand on Maddie's arm. "You want me to wait here or come on up? Or be on my way?"

"If you really wouldn't mind, I'd kind of like you there when I look at the results."

"Sure thing, hon. Whatever the results, just know I'll help you through this while you're in the UK, no matter what you decide. In this day and age, a woman's got options in these types of situations."

Maddie gripped her hand on the spired fence by the hotel and waited for a wave of nausea to pass. As a double-decker red bus idled at the nearby bus stop, the smell of exhaust made her feel even sicker. She sipped some water, took a deep breath, and turned to face Dot. "I don't have any moral objections to a woman terminating a pregnancy, but I'm not sure that's the route I want to take."

Dot draped her arm around Maddie's shoulders. "I didn't necessarily mean that option. I guess what I'm trying to say is that you don't have to say yes to Drew's proposal. He can certainly be a part of the baby's life, if that's what you want, but you needn't marry him out of obligation."

Maddie stared at the sidewalk. "I grew up with only a mother. My mom's boyfriend ended up being like a father to me, but that wasn't until I was in high school. I often wonder how different my life would've been if I'd had a father there from the start. If it does turn out that I'm pregnant, I'd want my child to grow up with a complete parental unit."

Dot walked up the steps to the hotel entrance and opened the door. "Maybe we oughta get a definitive answer before you go making any big decisions."

Maddie trudged up the three flights of stairs toward her room, each step moving her closer to an uncertain future. Aware of her options, Maddie's mind raced as she tried her best to stay in the here and now, but one thing she knew for certain was that she did love Drew, no matter how she still felt about exploring her sexuality.

Once in the hotel room, Dot plopped on the bed, and Maddie locked herself in the bathroom. She removed the stick from the package and read the instructions. Peeing on a stick was an awkward experience, and setting it carefully on the basin was surreal.

But the worst part was waiting for the result. She slumped to the floor, angry and disappointed that she'd gotten herself into this situation. She'd sat through an entire semester of health classes. She knew the risks of unprotected sex. Yet she'd allowed herself to get carried away in a moment of pleasure with Drew, and now look what had happened.

"Well?" Dot said from behind the door. "What's the verdict?"

Maddie wasn't brave enough to look at the stick, so she opened the door and held it up for Dot to read.

"Right, just as you probably thought." Dot pulled Maddie into a tight embrace.

When she caught a glimpse of the blue plus sign on the pregnancy test, Maddie's eyes filled with tears. After she pulled away from Dot's hug, she stepped to the window and set her hand on the phone. There, next to the telephone was the postcard she'd written to Ally but hadn't mailed yet. Maddie shuffled the postcard into a pile of London brochures and reached for her calling card. She punched in the numbers of her calling card but paused before entering Drew's number. When she realized it was only four a.m. back home, she hung up and slumped on the bed next to Dot and started to sob. Without saying a word, Dot wrapped an arm around Maddie and held her close.

Just one day prior, Maddie's life had been so different as she wandered around London and then met Erika at the dance club. Like a bird testing her wings, Maddie felt free on the dance floor. Though she longed to feel Erika's lips on hers once again, she couldn't see her tonight or tomorrow. Not after this. Not ever again.

Maddie reached for the phone and entered Erika's number, prepared to give her some lame excuse about needing to cancel their date. When she got Erika's voicemail, Maddie almost hung up. But she took a deep breath before speaking. "Hey, this is Maddie. I hate to cancel our date at the last minute, but something's come up. I'm really sorry." She hung up the phone and stared out the window and started to cry once again.

Maddie would call Drew in a couple hours to tell him the news, but right now she made the decision to not hyphenate her name, to refuse to be called Mrs. Drew Richards, and to instead go by Maddie Fong Richards. Drew would make a great father and would be dedicated and loving to both her and the baby. But Mad-

die's wings had been clipped. From here on out, she would have
to ignore the desires that still burned inside her.

Chapter Twenty

Laguna Beach, California: February 2002

Now that Mom, Kai, and Drew had gone home, Maddie cherished this time alone with her baby girl. From her fourth-floor room of the hospital, Maddie had a clear view of the golden rays of sunlight filtering through the grey clouds over the ocean. The skies had been dark and stormy for the past few days, but the sun finally peeked through the clouds this afternoon.

Maddie gazed at the sleeping infant in her arms—amazed that she and Drew had created this precious newborn. Drew had been by Maddie's side since yesterday morning. She'd been full of fear when she went into labor, but fortunately, it was short and fairly easy with minimal pain once they gave her an epidural. Her baby was fed and sleeping for now, but the nurse told her it wouldn't be long before she woke up again.

With her swaddled baby nestled in her arms, Maddie finally had a chance to properly admire the flowers and gifts from loved ones. A big bouquet of pink roses and peonies from Drew sat on the table next to the bed; various tropical arrangements sent from Kai's relatives in Hawaii were displayed on the ledge under the window. An array of cards and stuffed animals lined the shelf below the television. A huge purple Mylar balloon with the words "It's a girl!" hovered over Maddie's head.

The best gifts arrived this afternoon by FedEx. Dot sent a onesie with an image of Virginia Woolf on the front that she'd painted and transferred onto the soft cotton material. Along with the cute outfit, Dot enclosed a children's book by Woolf titled *The Widow and the Parrot* and a quote printed on lavender paper displayed in a wooden frame that Dot carved out of mahogany. Maddie recognized the quote from one of Woolf's earliest short stories—the message perfect for the first few years of her daughter's life:

Once she knows how to read there's only one thing you can teach her to believe in and that is herself—Virginia Woolf, from "A Society."

Touched that Dot sent these gifts overnight, Maddie flipped through the children's book and read a few pages aloud. After setting the book down on the bed, she leaned over to kiss the baby's little head and ran her fingers over the soft dark ringlets. Even though the infant was only a day old, Maddie already felt a deep connection.

While she gazed at the baby's sleeping face, someone entered the room. Maddie looked up to see Ally standing there with a bouquet of red roses in her arms. Maddie's mouth flung open, but no words came out. Ally lingered in the doorway but didn't say a word, not quite meeting Maddie's eyes.

Maddie's hands got sweaty, and her face broke into a smile. "This is such a great surprise." Maddie felt that same fluttery sensation she experienced years ago whenever she was around Ally and quickly remembered why she'd once fallen in love with her. Ally's warm smile and beautiful eyes reminded Maddie of what they experienced when they were younger. They hadn't kissed that long ago, but to Maddie it seemed like a lifetime.

Ally remained by the door but finally looked at Maddie. "As I drove down here, I got more and more excited at the thought of seeing you. Well, and to meet your baby. But as I neared the hospital, I almost turned around and headed back to L.A."

Maddie watched her baby girl sleep peacefully in her arms and thought carefully of what to say. Were there any words that could bridge the distance between her and Ally? When Maddie gazed at Ally's beautiful face, her heart beat a little faster. "I'm glad you didn't turn around. How'd you find out I had the baby?"

Ally stepped closer to the bed and looked at the sleeping infant in Maddie's arms. "Kai called me last night and encouraged me to come down here today."

"I'm surprised my mom didn't send out a mass email to let everyone know."

"Well, she did do that early this morning." Ally laughed and sat on the edge of the bed. "What a beautiful baby. This kid's gonna get an abundance of love from a mom like you."

"And from her dad." Maddie averted her gaze from Ally's. "Drew's been amazing these past few months. He didn't even have any reservations about me wanting to name the baby Taylor. If she'd been a boy, I would've named him Samuel."

When Ally smiled, her eyes lit up. "Taylor is a perfect name for her."

Maddie had settled on the name Taylor while she was reading a book of Coleridge's poems for her British literature class. Though hip and modern, the name would always be a link to Ally.

Maddie gazed at her precious baby in her arms and then looked at Ally. "No one but you and I will know the true significance of why I named her after Samuel Taylor Coleridge."

As Ally looked at Taylor asleep in Maddie's arms, her eyes filled with tears. "As Coleridge once wrote, 'Oh sleep, it is a gentle thing.'"

"When I was pregnant, I read 'The Rime of the Ancient Mariner' aloud a few times. It's not exactly a lullaby, but I wanted to expose her to literature even before she was born. Of course, Drew spent many hours playing classical music while this little one was inside the womb. Once she's old enough, I'll take her to the beach and teach her to swim and then to surf."

"Knowing you, she'll be in the water even before she learns to walk."

"With so many surfers in the family, Taylor will definitely grow up being in or near the ocean. Maybe she'll end up being a pro surfer like I'd planned to do." Maddie smiled as she fought back the tears.

Though filled with elation to have this baby in her arms, Maddie couldn't stop the tears from flowing. Ever since she gave birth yesterday, her emotions were out of whack—feeling euphoric one moment, then crying the next. In one moment, things seemed totally clear, and then a few minutes later, she was wrought with uncertainty. But whenever she looked at Taylor asleep in her arms, she was brought back to the here and now. Maddie's future remained fuzzy except for the certainty that she'd make sure Taylor had the best life possible.

And Ally was right. Taylor would be in the ocean way before she learned to walk. After she taught Taylor how to swim and then to read, Maddie would spend the next several years showing her how to believe in herself.

Without saying a word, Ally sat closer to Maddie and wiped the tears from her cheeks. The old familiar tug of attraction arose, but Maddie resisted the urge to kiss Ally.

By now, it was totally dark outside. The early winter sunset had left the sky completely black. For a couple minutes, they didn't say a word as they stared at the sleeping infant in Maddie's arms. The silence was familiar and comforting. Exhausted but exhilarated to have this new life nestled against her chest, Maddie couldn't take her eyes off Taylor.

As she gazed at Taylor, Maddie's heart opened up even more, but she couldn't stop crying—deep wrenching sobs that seemed to have no end. Ally wrapped her arm around Maddie. She kissed her on the forehead and reached over to hold her hand. The sobs finally subsided. Maddie hesitantly let go of Ally's hand to grab a handful of tissues and wipe her face. She inhaled and exhaled, slowly and deeply. Now she was ready to talk again.

"I'm glad you didn't change your mind about seeing me tonight." Maddie said the words quietly but gave Ally a warm smile. "It's nice having you here with me right now. It seemed weird to go through this pregnancy without you nearby. Not a day went by that I didn't miss you." As she did her best to not break down even more, Maddie snuggled closer to Ally.

Ally dabbed her eyes with a tissue. "I missed you, too. I was stupid to run from such a good thing and to never have told you that I loved you."

"Well, I never exactly told you that I loved you. At least not out loud. I guess I always figured words weren't necessary to convey how I felt about you."

Ally wiped a tear from her cheek. "I'd actually planned to tell you how I felt about you in June when I was in France. I mean, had you come over to visit. Even my mom helped me plan it all out. You know my mom. She's a little over the top sometimes. I'd just planned to talk to you while we strolled next to the Seine at sunset, but my mom suggested I get a bottle of wine, cheese, bread, and a special French pastry for dessert."

Maddie stared at her in shock. "Your *mom* helped you with the plans?"

"Yeah, she's the one who suggested I take you to this really awesome spot along the Seine, right next to a park."

"So, your mom knows about us...or about what we had at one time?" Maddie's heart raced as she took all of this in.

"I told my parents a few weeks before our trip to France about us...and how I still felt about you. My dad was kind of weird about it at first, but my mom wasn't surprised at all. She even said she'd seen how happy I was whenever you were around but never said anything, especially since I ended up dating a couple guys…including Colin."

Maddie shook her head and sighed loudly as she fought back the tears. She couldn't even look at Ally. For a couple awkward moments, neither of them said a word as they stared at Taylor, asleep in Maddie's arms.

Ally set her hand on Maddie's arm. "I don't blame you for hating me for what I did. It was shitty of me to get involved with Colin in the first place when I knew how you felt about me. I mean, your cousin, of all people. He's a nice guy, but he and I never connected when it came to important things like literature. Same with the other guys I dated. None of them were all that supportive of me being so into photography…like you were."

Maddie finally looked at Ally. "I don't hate you. I never did. I was hurt, but I guess I figured you realized you were into guys and just moved on from what we had."

"Well, I thought that's what I wanted. When I was in Paris, I had this whole elaborate speech rehearsed in my head, things I wanted to finally say to you."

"There were so many times when I was in London that I thought about you. The end of that trip was awful. I even came home a few days early. Then I didn't even have the decency to let you know why I couldn't visit you in France." Maddie's eyes welled up with tears. She knew what happened in London was behind her and that she couldn't go back, but she didn't want to tell Ally anything more about that trip. Erika would always be an amazing memory of her time in London, but that was all she'd ever be.

"It's okay. It all makes sense now why you couldn't meet up with me in France."

"We're quite the pair, huh? But we sure did have some good times." Maddie wiped the tears from her face. She looked at the flowers in Ally's hands and narrowed her eyes. "Are those…Valentine's Day flowers? If so, you're a couple weeks early."

"More like a couple years late." Ally set the flowers on the table next to the bed. "I always wanted to give you roses. I never imagined it would be to congratulate you on the birth of your baby, but I guess I should've brought a vase." Ally glanced at the other bouquets on the ledge under the window.

"You drove all the way down here to bring me flowers? You

could've had them delivered like most people did." Not sure what else to say, Maddie let out a nervous laugh. "I've always loved red roses. I guess for now we can put them in the vase with the pink flowers until Mom can bring a vase from home."

"I wasn't about to have flowers delivered when I could bring them to you myself." Ally removed the cellophane from the roses and added them to the pink flowers. "You've got quite an assortment of flowers here. I'm guessing the pink ones are from your husband. My red roses look so bright next to Drew's flowers."

For a moment, Maddie studied the red roses mixed in with Drew's pink flowers. "You're right that the pink flowers are from Drew, but…he's not my husband."

Ally's mouth opened, but she didn't say a word for a few seconds. She looked at Maddie and cocked her head. "Did you decide to wait and get married after the baby was born?"

Though hardly anyone knew the details of why Maddie opted to not marry Drew, she was always discreet when she explained what happened. "Drew's a great guy, and I know he'll be an amazing father to Taylor, but I finally realized I couldn't stay with him."

"So, you two aren't together? You're not…planning to marry him?"

"I'll always love Drew but…not in the way that a wife should love her husband. He and I will be closely connected as we raise Taylor, but we have no plans to live together. At least not in the foreseeable future. For now, I'm still living with Mom and Kai. Drew's got a place of his own in San Clemente, so Taylor will see him as often as possible."

"I assumed you were happily married and excited to start a family with Drew. What changed? Not that being a single mom is wrong."

Maddie took a deep breath and stared at the ceiling. "Before I realized I was pregnant, I was pretty much ready to finally live life as a lesbian. Or, at least explore what I'd kept buried for a long time. Then, fate intervened. After I got back from England, I realized it was wrong to marry Drew just because I was having his baby."

"How did Drew take it when you told him you didn't want to get married?"

"He was disappointed and tried to get me to reconsider, but

once he realized I definitely didn't want to get married, he respected my decision. Even though I knew I wanted to date women, I figured it'd be better to remain single. Besides, I doubt anyone would want to date a young mother with a newborn. Probably best to stay single."

"Well, you never know. I bet there are lots of great women out there who'd love both you and Taylor, but…sometimes being single helps us figure out what we really want. At least that's how it's been for me over the past several months."

For a few moments, they didn't say a word. Maddie heard the murmur of voices in the hallway. She closed her eyes and thought about what Ally said.

Ally scooted closer to Maddie. "When I drove down here to see you, I was thinking about how I wasn't sure what I wanted. I mean, as far as who I ended up with down the road. Even though I dated some sweet guys, I realized that…well, I didn't feel any sort of passion with them like I did with you. Then I thought about how I should just focus on starting law school and moving forward as far as a career in law. I've been planning to apply to Northwestern. I figured I might as well pick up where my brother left off."

"Sounds like lots of changes are in store for both of us. That's exciting that you might be going to law school at Northwestern."

Ally averted her eyes from Maddie's and clasped her hands in her lap. "Illinois seems so far from Southern California…and far from a lot of great things." Ally reached for Maddie's hand and looked at her with such sadness in her eyes. "I hope you know I never meant to hurt you. I just never expected to fall in love when I was so young. The way I felt about you scared me, and I guess I wasn't sure how to handle it. It's not like I had anyone to talk to about it."

With Ally's hand in hers, a calm washed over Maddie. The moments of confusion and longing she experienced after Ally abruptly cut things off disappeared and were replaced by a sweet and enduring love. "When we were together, or whatever we were at the time, you had me to talk to, but… I get it. I mean, I too wasn't sure what to make of the intense feelings I had for you."

"Intense is a perfect word for it." Ally let out a quiet sob and dabbed her eyes with a tissue. "The thing is, years ago I was scared and really immature. Also, when my feelings for you went from infatuation to love, I realized I wasn't sure I was ready to be in a relationship with a woman." That familiar pensive look that Maddie always loved washed over Ally's face. "What I do know is that I loved you years ago…and still do."

Maddie tried to calm her breathing, hardly able to believe what she'd just heard. "What are you saying?"

"Here with you now, things couldn't be clearer to me. I want to be with you. I was such an idiot to run from you. Like I said in my email to you, being away in France gave me a lot of time to think about things. Maddie, I love you."

Maddie ran her finger over Taylor's soft cheek. "Ally, I have a newborn. You've got law school in the near future."

"I'm no longer sure I want to get into law. I might end up staying in L.A. to pursue what I've always loved. A gallery near UCLA wants to display and sell some of my photos. For once, I think I might follow my heart and not my head."

Maddie looked deep into Ally's eyes—the same eyes that captivated her years ago when she first fell in love with her. "L.A. is a whole lot closer than Illinois."

Ally ran her fingers through Maddie's hair and kissed her on the cheek. "Maddie, I don't ever want to lose you again or let you go. When I thought you were gonna marry Drew, I figured I should just be happy that we had what we had and stop dwelling on how I should've never let you go, but here with you now, I know for sure I want to be with you."

Though she enjoyed Ally's touch, Maddie pulled away. How could she trust what Ally said? Why would things be different now compared to before? Maddie couldn't stop her body from trembling. "I never stopped loving you, but you have to understand that my life is complicated now. I've got a baby and will be co-parenting with Drew. We've agreed to always live nearby so Taylor can see both of us as much as possible—at least until she starts school. If Drew ends up getting a really great job in another city, I might even move to wherever he does."

Ally's smile faded for a brief moment, and she bit her lower lip. She set her hand on Maddie's arm. "We'll make it work. I'm sure Taylor's got two sets of grandparents who'd love to babysit while we go out on a date."

Ally's touch sent shivers through Maddie's body. Maddie couldn't ignore the heat that surged deep inside. "I bet they'd even agree to babysit for the weekend…like, if you and I went away together. Drew's grandparents have a beach house in Morro Bay. Might be a nice getaway for us once Taylor is a bit older. Maybe I could bring my board and check out the waves up there."

Ally smiled, her expression as playful as it was in their youth. "I've missed waiting for you on shore as you surf. Watching you ride the waves, seeing you in your bikini… Those images have flashed through my mind so many times since we last kissed."

"After having a baby, I'm not exactly in the best shape to be in a bikini. I gained over twenty pounds when I was pregnant."

"You'll always be sexy and beautiful to me. I want to finally explore your body and show you how I feel about you."

Maddie ached with longing at Ally's words. She wanted that so badly. But her life was more complicated now. "It might be a while until we can…be together in that way."

Ally set her hand on Maddie's cheek and kissed her softly on the lips. "I'll wait as long as necessary, but I don't ever want to hide how I feel about you again."

The familiarity of Ally's lips was a reminder of a simpler time when adult decisions didn't loom in the near future, of the days when nothing mattered except simple moments like this. With one kiss not being enough, Maddie pressed her lips against Ally's once more. Their kisses quickly became more passionate—Ally's lips and tongue awakening something in Maddie that'd been dormant for a while. After Ally pulled away, she stared deep into Maddie's eyes, as if she had more to say.

Though she too had more to say, Maddie remained silent. Right now, with her baby in her arms and Ally by her side, this moment was perfect. There would be lots of obstacles in the way as she adjusted to being a mom. But for now, this was all that mattered. She rested her head on Ally's shoulder and closed her eyes. For the first time in a long while, Maddie felt safe and less uncertain about the future. There were exciting adventures ahead—with new surf breaks to explore and more waves to catch.

About the Author

Lynnette Beers has been telling stories ever since she was a child, but it wasn't until adulthood that she realized she wanted to pursue a career in writing. After earning degrees in English and film studies, she went on to get an MA in literature and an MFA in fiction writing. She's been a professor of writing and literature for over twenty-five years. In addition to writing fiction, she writes narrative essays and academic papers. As a member of the International Virginia Woolf Society, she has presented papers at conferences in the US and UK. Her first book, *Just Beyond the Shining River*, was a Goldie finalist for best debut novel and was also recognized by Woolf Society members for paying homage to Virginia Woolf. She's also the author of the romance-intrigue novel, titled *Saving Sam*. In the summer of 2019, she was a writer in residence on the island of Molokai where she spent a few weeks immersing herself in Hawaiian culture while working on a historical novel set in Hawaii in the mid-1940s.

Lynnette lives in a coastal town in Southern California where she enjoys mountain biking, hiking, and ocean swimming. She grew up in San Diego County where she learned early on to respect the power of the ocean.

Website: lynnettebeers.com
Twitter: @BeersLynnette
Follow her on Facebook: Lynnette Beers Author
Follow her on Instagram: @lynnettebeers

Books by Lynnette Beers

Just Beyond the Shining River

After she gave up a promising career as an artist and turned her back on her British roots, Gemma Oldfield settled into life in Los Angeles to be with the woman who'd captured her heart. When things don't go as planned, Gemma buries herself in her work as a Hollywood set decorator–all the while clinging to the hope that the passion with her lover can be rekindled. But she must temporarily leave L.A. behind and return to England after her grandmother's unexpected passing.

Once there, she discovers shocking secrets she could never have foreseen. When she finds hundreds of letters written from a mysterious person dating as far back as the 1930s, Gemma embarks upon a quest to understand why her grandmother took so many secrets to her grave.

In her pursuit to learn more about her grandmother's past, Gemma meets an intriguing woman who has the potential to change the course of her life forever. But can Gemma open her heart to love again? Will she stay in England for a new beginning or return to the States to the life she knew before?

Saving Sam

As an experienced San Diego lifeguard, Sam Cleveland has been trained to save others. On what becomes the most treacherous beach day ever, she battles the sea as her ability as a lifeguard is tested. While she risks her life to rescue swimmers from the rough surf, her world comes crashing down when she learns that her brother Robert has been in a serious accident. She then must leave San Diego and the young woman she's recently started dating to return to her hometown—a place that holds a horrid memory from her childhood.

Once back in Mississippi, Sam sits vigil at Robert's bedside. Always protective when Sam was a child, Robert clings to life as investigators search for the person responsible for his accident. As she faces the possibility of losing her brother, Sam is reminded that her hometown holds an unspeakable secret that she and Robert vowed to always keep buried.

On the hunt for the man who intentionally harmed Robert is Lieutenant Annie Wright—the woman who captured Sam's heart years ago. Now just friends, Sam and Annie work together to find the person responsible for Robert's injuries. But as painful childhood memories resurface, so do old feelings of love. Will Sam choose to move forward with the chance at new romance in San Diego, or will she return to the comfort of familiar love with Annie in Mississippi?

Bringing Rainbow Stories to Life

Visit us at our website: www.flashpointpublications.com

www.ingramcontent.com/pod-product-compliance
Lightning Source LLC
Chambersburg PA
CBHW071806190726
48292CB00008B/2727